C000161559

STRAYS

A NOVEL BY

JENNIFER CALOYERAS

strays

a novel by

Jennifer Caloyeras

Ashland Creek Press

Strays
A Novel by Jennifer Caloyeras

Published by Ashland Creek Press
Ashland, Oregon
www.ashlandcreekpress.com

© 2015 Jennifer Caloyeras
All rights reserved. No part of this book may be reproduced or transmitted, in any
form or by any means, without written permission of the publisher.

ISBN 978-1-61822-037-0
Library of Congress Control Number: 2014949308

Printed in the United States of America on acid-free paper. All paper products used
to create this book are Sustainable Forestry Initiative (SFI) Certified Sourcing. Cover
design by Matt Smith (www.lilroundhouse.com).

This is a work of fiction. Names, characters, places, and incidents either are the
product of the author's imagination or are used fictiously, and any resemblance to
actual persons, living or dead, businesses, companies,
events, or locales is entirely coincidental.

For my parents, Ron and Sheila

And for my four-legged friends: Tips, Reba, Willie, and Dingo—all good dogs

prologue

I brought the hammer down as hard as I could and watched the stucco of my closet wall crumble. That was for being dumped by Andy Dunn. I raised the wooden handle over my head and brought it down again with even more force—a human guillotine. That was for Mrs. Schneider's condescending remark in English class. Another bash for my dad for being too busy to deal with me. A slam for my so-called best friend, Ashley, for not calling me back the night before. And a smash for my mom—for dying—that sent bits of drywall flying.

I waited until my chest stopped its rhythmic heaving up and down, like the waves of the Pacific that I could see from my bedroom window. After rearranging my clothing on the hangers so that they hid all evidence of my outburst, I stepped out of the closet and closed the doors. As usual, the hammering had been therapeutic. I had let it all out.

Or so I thought.

one

I couldn't ignore them any longer. It was one thing to walk around the school cafeteria hiding behind my sunglasses, pretending I didn't see them waving at me, but they knew I hadn't gone deaf, so when my two "friends" started shouting my name, I had to walk over.

"Iris!" yelled Ashley again, both hands in the air like she was on a roller coaster. She had been my closest friend, if you could call it that, since I had moved to Santa Cruz, California, to start my sophomore year less than two years ago.

Sierra followed with a bellowing, "Eye!"

Eye was their nickname for me, but I never had the heart to tell them they should stick to Iris because calling me by the first letter of my name kind of creeped me out. I just always pictured this big, ominous eye hovering over my head.

I don't know why they'd plucked me out of all the girls at Santa Cruz High. It wasn't like I had been giving out signals that I wanted to hang out. In fact, I spent most of that first year in tenth grade with my head down, hiding behind my long brown hair. Maybe they were intrigued by the new girl with the tragic past.

Begrudgingly, I brought my sack lunch over.

"For a second there, I thought you were avoiding us," said Sierra, who was clearly breaking the dress code by sporting a tube top.

"I wouldn't do that," I lied. Truth was, I had been craving more and more time alone with my thoughts lately. But it was hard to explain this to my friends because I couldn't even really understand it myself. After finally settling in to a new home and my new life without Mom, I found myself wanting to retreat, as though the comfort scared me. I was shying away, like a hamster or a jaguar, from being a social creature.

It finally felt like the beginning of summer—the kind of day that made people visiting Santa Cruz announce to their families that they were moving to California immediately. Outside, a cerulean sky with rising heat made me envy all of the kids downing cool sodas. Dad had forgotten to give me my allowance this morning, so I was stuck with a boring peanut butter and jelly sandwich from home. And drinking fountain water—lukewarm.

"You look tired," Ashley said as I sat down.

"I woke up late, and Dad drank all the coffee this morning," I said.

"Coffee stunts your growth," said Sierra. She was going to end up at least six feet tall, like her brothers, and no amount of caffeine could stop her.

"Well, it also staves off type-two diabetes," I added.

"Here she goes," said Sierra.

That shut me up. I didn't have to subject them to my Science Channel addiction.

I could feel the crunchy peanut bits sticking to my teeth. "How'd you do on bio?" I asked, trying to change the subject.

"There's no way anyone got the extra credit on the bio final this morning. No way," said Sierra, opening her plastic container filled with noodles. She was a senior who sometimes hung out with us.

Since I was in accelerated science, we were in the same class.

The sides of my mouth turned upward, ever so subtly.

"What was the question?" asked Ashley.

Sierra used her teeth to rip open the package of soy sauce. "It was something like: 'What's special about the way moray eels eat?'"

"And 'What is this mechanism called?'" I added.

"I'm glad I'm not in any of those AP classes," said Ashley.

"Why would Mr. Sommers even include extra credit questions if they're impossible to answer? It's cruel," said Sierra.

My smile widened, and Ashley glanced over at me. It was one of the few pleasures I had experienced in months. I wanted to revel in it.

Ashley was onto me. "You got it, didn't you?" she said.

"She's smart, but she's not *that* smart," said Sierra, studying my eyes as my pupils widened. "Oh my God. You did get it. What in the world was the answer?"

I gave them the full explanation. "Moray eels have a second set of jaws at the back of their mouths. They're called *pharyngeal jaws*, and when the eel clamps down on its prey, the second set protrudes forward to help bring the food back into the esophagus."

Ashley put down her burrito. "I think I'm gonna puke."

"Where in the world did you learn that? Mr. Sommers never even covered that in class," said Sierra.

"He didn't talk about it in class. It was on one of those nature programs I watch."

I could get so caught up in those shows that hours would pass and I wouldn't even notice. And since I'd been feeling so antisocial lately, my propensity for marathon sessions of TV watching had increased significantly.

"You kind of have a photographic memory," said Ashley.

"No, I don't," I said. "Only when it comes to things…" I paused, thinking about what I was trying to say. What was the information I was more likely to remember?

"Related to animals?" Ashley offered.

"I guess. I remember some flora stuff, too, but mostly the fauna," I said.

"You should try going to the Monterey Bay Aquarium with her. It's like having your own personal tour guide," said Ashley.

I guess I had been a bit much when we took a road trip forty-five minutes south to Monterey soon after we met. It had been a kind gesture for Ashley to invite me along with her family, and Dad had been happy to spend the weekend holed up in his office. Ashley had made fun of me for spouting off facts and strange trivia about the various sea animals—they were my specialty. With all the time I had spent in the ocean, I felt a bit like a sea animal myself. At least I used to feel that way. The ocean now reminded me too much of my mom, so I avoided it. But whenever I heard or read anything about an animal—it didn't matter what kind—the fact would get filed away in my head, and I could recall it at any given moment.

"Wonder why it doesn't work with everything?" asked Sierra.

I had been wondering the same thing. I had four more finals to take over the next week, and only the easiest one—biology—was behind me. I was pretty sure I had nailed it. But the rest of the week would bring precalculus, Spanish 3, AP U.S. history, and the most dreaded one: English 3. It was my only class that wasn't advanced, which was ironic because my mom had been a librarian who was basically in love with books. I'd been doing okay in English until I was placed in Mrs. Schneider's class last year, in the tenth grade. And then, as luck would have it, I got her again the following year.

Schneider was like a virus I could not shake.

She approached English like an army lieutenant—all rules and no fun. Above her desk was a quote by Molière: GRAMMAR, WHICH KNOWS HOW TO CONTROL EVEN KINGS. But Schneider ran her classroom like King Henry the Eighth—hacking off our proverbial heads every time anyone misspoke.

I knew I should have been studying more, working harder to make sure I kept up my 3.8 grade point average, but the more I studied "the rules," the more mottled they became.

Looking around the cafeteria, you could see severe cases of "senioritis" everywhere. Students were constantly talking about what colleges they were going to, pushing the limits of the already pretty lax dress code in the form of too-short skirts, and exuding a joy that I did not share.

High school was so compartmentalized. You could see it in the yearbook: who the sporty kids were, the skaters, the nerds, the theater geeks, the popular kids. But my friends seemed to transcend that kind of labeling. We were part of different things at school. Sierra wrote for the school newspaper, *The Weekly Slug*; Ashley played volleyball; and I sang in the choir and was part of the school science team that met over an occasional lunch period to discuss the latest breaking news. We were an eclectic trio.

"One week until we're seniors!" I said with fake enthusiasm, trying to take the focus off me and the inner workings of my weird brain.

"I know—I can't believe it! Next year is going to be so awesome!" said Ashley.

Mom had always talked about the importance of getting into a good college, which felt kind of weird because Dad had never gone. He'd worked his way from construction worker to contractor to businessman, all without a degree. But Mom was always so nostalgic about her college days at Brown University, it was only natural that I would follow in her footsteps.

Dad would always debate with her. "We have some fine state schools in California."

But she'd fire back, "It's not the same as being hunkered down in the dead of winter in a library that's been in operation for over two hundred years."

And that was the image I conjured most often when I pictured myself at college: sitting bundled in a cold library with a long knit sweater, surrounded by books on molecular biology. I realized not every junior romanticized college in quite the same way.

After Mom died, Dad and I didn't really talk about college plans anymore. He had thrown himself into his new job, and I was busy figuring out if and how I was going to make new friends. But when I came home one day last year with a Brown brochure that the college counselor had given me, Dad sat me down and expressed his concerns.

"We can't afford it."

I knew there was one less income coming in, which was why our new duplex in Santa Cruz was way smaller than our house in Topanga Canyon, just north of Los Angeles.

"I'm a good student. I can get a scholarship."

"It's not that simple," he said. "We're not poor enough for a scholarship."

So there I was, not rich enough to afford a private university, but not poor enough for assistance—stuck between a rock and a hard place. Stuck with Dad in California. The good news was my grades had been strong—at least until this semester—and I'd been slowly adding to my nest egg with the funds I'd received from Mom's small trust. The money was accumulating a modest amount of interest at First Pacific Bank. What better way to spend it than on my education? I knew she'd approve of my plan. With that money there, my college counselor explained, I could qualify for a loan.

"So, what does it feel like to have one more week until graduation?" Ashley asked Sierra. More than anything, I wanted to switch places with Sierra and officially be a high school graduate.

"I can't wait to get out of this place," said Sierra. "I mean, Santa Cruz is pretty and all, but doesn't it make you feel like the world is so much bigger? There are colleges with student populations as big as this entire city!"

"Seriously? Like where?" Ashley asked.

"Ohio State, for one." Sierra had had her heart set on that school since the beginning of last year. It was all we ever heard about. We were glad when her acceptance letter finally arrived in the mail. "Can you imagine all the single guys there will be to choose from? And I'm not talking surfer types."

It was true. Our city boasted an inordinately high ratio of surfer guys: tanned skin; long, sun-bleached hair; and this laid-back attitude that made you feel that even if you took one by surprise and slapped him across the face, he'd just keep the conversation rolling.

"Um, speaking of which," said Sierra. "Looks like Andy found himself a freshman."

We turned our heads in unison to see what Sierra was talking about, making it totally obvious that we were spying on Andy Dunn—my ex. Not surprisingly, he was one of those surfer types, but with a brain. He had broken up with me two weeks earlier. He said that I just seemed closed off, that I wasn't letting him in. He claimed he meant emotionally, but I had an entirely different interpretation; I hadn't been ready to do much more than kiss him. We'd dated for three months, and seeing him with another girl made my stomach ache in its lowest depths.

"Whatever," I said, turning back around, pretending to shrug the whole thing off. But *the waters were rising*—or at least that's how I felt as the anger gained momentum in my body. I tried to ignore the feeling by anticipating the damage I would inflict on my closet wall once I got home.

"You mean, that doesn't bug you?" Sierra pointed straight at them.

"You don't have to point," Ashely said, lowering Sierra's arm.

"He can do what he wants. Fine by me," I lied.

It wasn't fine. The last thing I wanted was a front-row seat to their face-sucking festival. How insensitive could one person be? And to think I'd actually loved this guy. Or, at least I thought I had.

I changed the subject. "So what are the official summer plans?"

"Summer school if I didn't pass my biology final," said Sierra.

"You'll pass," I said. So much of my time was spent telling these two that they were pretty or skinny or that they'd pass or whatever else they wanted to hear. It was exhausting.

"Okay, supposing I pass AP bio," said Sierra, "I guess summer will be spent being a junior counselor at Summer Brooke Day Camp in Los Gatos, packing up for college, and then hanging with you fine people each afternoon, right?"

"You guys are so lucky," said Ashley. "I have to work."

"Yeah, at the best coffee house in Santa Cruz!" I couldn't hide my excitement that Ashley would be behind the counter at Pergolesi, a Victorian-house-turned-coffee-shop where college students went to study. She had already assured me that as long as her manager wasn't around, I could have all the free coffee I wanted.

"You're working, too, right, Eye?" asked Sierra.

"Babysitting. Same boys I sit during the week sometimes."

I would be babysitting the Harrison boys from nine to three every day. Their mom worked some part-time computer-type job over the hill in San Jose and made enough to pay me $15 an hour, a 25 percent raise from last summer. It was a pretty easy job, and even fun at times: walking the boys to the park and the library. Every paycheck would transform into college credits.

"Do you have to change diapers?" asked Sierra.

"I did last year. But Conor's three now. He's potty trained. I just have to give him a jelly bean every time it lands in the potty."

"Eew! You have to watch him pee!" said Sierra.

"I'm just there to make sure everything goes where it's supposed to go," I said.

"I am only having girls," said Ashley, putting her uneaten lunch away.

Sierra laughed. "You don't get to choose!"

"I thought there were *ways* of making it go one way or the other. Like positions or some tea you could drink." Ashley could be so naïve.

"Yeah, Make-a-Girl tea," I said. "Saw that one on sale at the market last week."

We all laughed.

"Okay, Ms. Biology Expert, so you tell us then. How is a baby's sex determined?" asked Sierra.

I hadn't really thought of it before. Just knew there was a fifty-fifty chance.

"Sorry, guys, I only do animals," I said.

"People don't count as animals?" asked Ashley.

"Well, I guess humans are the one animal I don't understand," I said, staring at Andy, who was still slobbering all over that freshman girl. *The waters began rising again.* It felt as though I were drowning a slow death and there was nothing I could do to save myself.

Sierra's phone pinged, and she looked down to read the text. "I can't believe this!"

"What?" I asked.

"I was supposed to drive to a concert in Berkeley this weekend to review a band for the newspaper, but now my mom's saying she needs the car because she just got invited to some spa getaway with *her* friends. I seriously hate her. I wish she were dead."

Even though I was looking down at my sandwich, I could feel their eyes on me, waiting for my reaction.

"Sorry, Eye," said Sierra.

There that monocle was, floating above me. Looking down on me. Singling me out.

Girl with the dead mother.

"It's okay!" I assured her. After all, it should have been okay, an offhand remark said in front of someone whose mom happened to be dead. Sierra hadn't meant to offend, I understood that—but, truth be told, whenever people mentioned their moms I ached a little inside. It seemed like a waste of time to want something I couldn't have. Dad was still single, always too busy with work for girlfriends, but even if he remarried and I gained a stepmother, whether good or evil, she'd never replace my real mom.

I did my best to smile and empathize with Sierra.

"My mom wants to take us on a girls' shopping trip to San Francisco next weekend," Ashley said. "You ladies in?"

Sierra squealed. "Yes!"

"Eye?" asked Ashley. I knew she was being generous with her offer, but I was desperate for some time alone.

"Maybe," I answered, unenthusiastically.

"Aw, come on. We need your dad's juice for the ride up!"

Dad was a manager at a juicing facility just north of Santa Cruz, and his one and only perk seemed to be a limitless supply of fresh-squeezed fruit and vegetable juices that filled our otherwise scant refrigerator to the brim.

"I'm totally going on a juice diet," said Sierra. "Tell your dad we need a case for the car. You have to come."

Did they only want me to go on the trip for my free drinks? I wondered if I put in a request like that whether Dad would bother following through—or even return my text, for that matter. He was always busy with work. When I was younger, he'd taken time off to go on vacations with me and my mom. We'd go camping in Yosemite or cross-country skiing in the Sierras. But after she died, Dad's workload seemed to increase, and I couldn't figure out whether he had actually been given more work or whether he had chosen to take it all on in order to avoid dealing with Mom's death—or dealing with me.

A wadded-up paper lunch bag hit Ashley in the face.

"Seriously?" she said. She picked it up and threw it back toward three boys at another lunch table, laughing. We didn't know their names but referred to them as Mutton Chop (the guy was always growing his sideburns), Streak (he had a streak of blond bleached at the front of his hair), and Hoodie Boy (who always wore the same hooded sweatshirt pulled tight so you could hardly see his face). All of them were troublemakers. They had been kicked out of class more times than I could count, and once in a while I'd see one of them sitting outside the principal's office, waiting, no doubt, for another stern warning. They were from a whole other world of kids who didn't listen, kids who had no college ambition, kids who would end up in the same place doing the same thing twenty years from now. Or worse: in jail.

"Here comes Principal C."

Principal Cagle was on the prowl again. Close to the end of the school year, he had a mission to bust anyone he could get his hands on, like he had some quota to fill. With the paper-bag delinquents only a table away, I didn't even question his steady pace toward us. Also, he and Ashley's dad were friends, and once in a while, just to make everyone feel awkward, he'd have a seat with us and start making small talk.

Sierra said, "Ashley, hide under the table, so he doesn't see you…"

Ashley was getting ready to squeeze under the laminate when Cagle leaned down toward me and said, not quite in a whisper, "Iris Moody, please meet me in my office in ten minutes."

My cheeks flushed as Cagle turned and walked away.

"He's so creepy," Sierra said, once he was out of earshot.

"What in the world was that about?" asked Ashley.

I shrugged.

"He probably just wants to tell you you've won some super-genius science award and they're etching your name on a plaque that will sit on the gym wall for all eternity," said Sierra.

The paper-bag boys were staring at me and laughing, still probably shocked that they weren't the ones Cagle was after.

"Want to walk around Pacific after school?" Sierra asked us.

Ashley nodded. "You'll come, too—right, Eye?" she asked.

"Sure," I said, less than enthusiastically. I really just wanted an afternoon to myself.

"Is everything okay?" Ashley asked.

"Peachy," I said in my perfected sarcastic tone.

Ashley rolled her eyes.

"You don't have to be rude about it," said Sierra.

"You guys have a good lunch," I said and grabbed my things. I just felt like being alone, wallowing in my funk. I told myself that once summer break officially started, I would emerge from hiding, ready to face the world.

As I walked toward Mr. Cagle's office, a nagging feeling took over my body that this meeting was going to be anything but congratulatory.

two

Waiting outside Principal Cagle's office was more nerve-racking than waiting at the dentist for a cavity to be filled. I had been seated on the same padded bench numerous times before, but always in anticipation of receiving some sort of accolade. In the middle of last year, I was ushered into his office so he could announce that I had been nominated for a science achievement award. And then, at the end of last year, my grades in science were so high that he sat me down and told me I could take AP biology in eleventh grade. This was the first time the school had made that sort of accommodation; it was a really big deal.

I thought about all of the reasons he could have summoned me. Did he know that I had tried to see Ms. Kaminsky, the school counselor, the day Andy dumped me? Had they been spying on me since I'd left her office pissed off because she had been too busy to make time for me? Had they been scrutinizing me, checking for signs of depression, studying the way I walked or which friends I hung out with? Or maybe it was my recently dipping grades. I wondered if it was Mrs. Schneider who had rallied for the meeting. I thought about the last time I had been in her class and I'd had the audacity to ask, "Can I go to the bathroom?"

"Surely you mean, *may I?*'"

My bladder couldn't have cared less about proper grammar.

Each time Mrs. Schneider called on me and I gave an incorrect answer, she would get this crazy look in her eyes, like she was longing for the days when she could whip out her switch and beat me across the top of my hands.

I sat on the bench in front of Mr. Cagle's office, staring at the big pot of coffee with a stack of paper cups next to it. It had obviously been put out for faculty or parents, but I pretended to be oblivious as I got up to help myself to a much-needed cup. But just as I brought the steaming liquid to my lips, the secretary, who looked like a recent college graduate, shook her head. I should have thrown it away. Instead, I downed it. It wasn't like she could send me to the principal's office.

"Mr. Cagle will see you now," squeaked the secretary.

Gathering my heavy messenger bag filled with books and binders, I turned the cool handle on Mr. Cagle's door.

I was greeted by an entire welcoming committee: Straight ahead was Mr. Cagle, sitting in his leather swivel chair; to my right was Ms. Kaminsky, the school counselor; and to my left—my biggest fear, old Mrs. Schneider.

Sabotaged.

The waters rose and the rage gathered in my throat. Had I been forced to speak at that moment, the words would have come out as a gurgle. Time seemed to slow down as I looked around the room at these people who had apparently been preparing my demise.

"Hi, Iris. Come on in and have a seat," Mr. Cagle said, as though he were inviting me to a garden party.

The only thing that possibly could have made this worse was if Dad had been there. I sat down.

"We've also asked your dad to join us. Any ideas where he might be?"

I couldn't believe this was happening. I should have studied more. I should have kept my grades up.

There was only one place Dad ever was.

"Work," I said.

"He confirmed his attendance, so hopefully he'll be joining us soon," said Mr. Cagle.

Dad had known about this meeting and had failed to tell me? I felt mortified. Betrayed. A little heads-up might have made this cozy get-together a little less shocking.

"So, Iris," began Ms. Kaminsky. She was young and wore a lot of eye makeup, like she had mistaken her day job for a beauty pageant. "I want you to know that this, right here, is a circle of safety, and anything that is said will be held in strict confidence."

Mrs. Schneider started coughing out of control. Maybe she had a tickle in her throat. Or maybe she was trying to hold back the laughter triggered by Ms. Kaminsky's comments. Schneider didn't seem like the type to believe in *circles of safety—circles of syntax* seemed more up her alley.

"Let's see here." Ms. Kaminsky riffled through a thick file. "It's been a rough few years for you."

Tears began welling up. It was the first time someone had publicly recognized that I'd been struggling, even though I had tried so hard to keep it all inside.

Ms. Kaminsky read through her paperwork. "Your parents divorced, your family moved, and then you had to deal with a pregnancy. Not easy things for a teenager."

What in the world was this woman talking about?

"Um, that's not me," I said. My tear ducts, which had threatened to flood like a broken levy, clamped shut.

Ms. Kaminsky flipped the file and checked the name on the front. "Oh, dear," she said. "This doesn't say Iris."

I shook my head.

"I am *so* sorry," she said. "I must have grabbed the wrong file." She looked at Mr. Cagle, embarrassed. His face remained stoic.

No, I'm the one with the dead mom, the boyfriend who dumped me, and the sinking grades, I wanted to say but didn't.

"Let's try to stay on track," said Mr. Cagle.

On track? Was this guy kidding? We were at two completely different train stations.

Mrs. Schneider looked like she couldn't stand any of this any longer. We'd obviously intruded on her lunchtime, which she probably spent crocheting miniature nooses that she would secretly wrap around voodoo versions of her students.

"The bottom line is, Iris, you're on the brink of failing English. You're no English scholar, but you have a good GPA, especially with all those accelerated math and science classes. But your grades are slipping, and we need to stop this downward spiral before you put your academic future at risk."

My heart hammered in my chest. I had just aced my bio final, and now this? Who had I become? How did I let this happen, and why did this trio suddenly care? I wondered what their real motivation was behind this meeting—genuine concern, or worry that their public funding would drop if they didn't have as many stellar students to boast about?

"Thank you, Mrs. Schneider." Mr. Cagle looked relieved that someone else had taken over. "Do you have anything you'd like to say, Iris?"

I wanted to tell him that English 3 was the most boring class I'd ever taken, that Schneider looked at us as though she wanted to kill us. How could I tell him that my heart was still broken after Andy had ripped it out and stomped on it with his surfboard? Or that Dad and I moved through the house, day in and day out, barely speaking a word to each other? How could they know what it was like to feel as though everyone always expected perfection from me, but I wasn't always able to deliver and was terrified of turning out to be a disappointment, and angry that I couldn't do anything to feel better?

They wouldn't understand any of it.

Just then, Dad breezed in, deep in conversation on his cell phone.

"Did you fix the problem with the time clock? Nah—it's an LCD display. Amano PIX-200. We need a new ribbon. And get some extra time cards while you're at it. We have a couple of busy weeks ahead of us before the conference."

Putting his long index finger up to the rest of us in the room, he signaled that he'd be off the phone in a minute. He finished the conversation with his back to the circle, the rest of us looking at one another, not quite sure how to handle the situation.

"There's really no cell phone use allowed." Mr. Cagle explained the policy to me as though it were my job to enforce it with my dad.

I put my hands up, resigned.

Dad finally finished his conversation, put his phone in his pocket, and sat down.

"Sorry about that," he said, but I didn't believe him.

Mr. Cagle explained the situation to my dad this time, mostly by plagiarizing Schneider's speech, causing Schneider's lips to purse as her hands formed into fists on her lap. When he finished and there was space in the air to talk, Dad looked at me and said, "I know Iris can do it. Right?"

What was I supposed to say to my dad? To the group? *I will memorize my prepositions. Cross my heart. I will learn to diagram sentences forwards and backwards.* What else was there to say but yes? *Yes, I will try harder. Yes, I will smile more. Yes, I will pretend that everything is all right just to make you people happy.*

"Yes," I said, to everyone but myself. Everyone seemed satisfied.

"Remember to use the study guide I handed out in class." Schneider reminded me of the fifteen-page document outlining all of the grammatical rules we were supposed to have memorized.

"We all believe in you, Iris," Mr. Cagle said.

He knew nothing about me.

Ms. Kaminsky then promised me that I could come by her office *"anytime* if you want to talk about *anything."*

Yeah, right.

Then there was Dad, sitting there scrolling through e-mails on his cell phone, probably thinking the same thing that was swimming through my head: *I'd rather be anywhere but here.*

"I have to rush back to work," said Dad after the meeting.

We were standing outside the administration building, and I had a paranoid feeling that every student who passed by was staring at me. I convinced myself that only Ashley and Sierra knew about my meeting with Mr. Cagle. And the paper-bag boys.

"You'll be okay," Dad told me with his fully clueless confidence.

I decided to skip out on afternoon choir. Nothing like trying to sing when you feel like all you want to do is cry. You end up sounding like a dying duck. The good thing about choir was that if you lost one player, it didn't really matter. According to Mr. Ortiz, our choir teacher, our voices were supposed to blend together. He wanted us to lose our identities. They wouldn't miss me.

Checking my cell phone at my locker, I saw that I had three texts. One from Ashley: *Are you still meeting us on Pacific at four?* One from Sierra: *Win another award?* And another one from Ashley: *What's going on?* Without responding, I deleted them all.

After gathering the necessary books, I unlocked my bike and rode to the one place I went when I wanted a retreat from my life: the beach.

❁

The wind whipped through my hair as my bike picked up speed. I had forgotten to apply salve, which meant my lips would probably be cracked and peeling by the end of the ride. But I didn't care.

I took a left on Water Street and sped down the hill. Every sixteen-year-old was dying to get behind the wheel of a car because it equaled freedom, but I'd had my independence for years with my bike.

I flew past a slew of old, colorful Victorian buildings, standard in this city, and past even more VW vans—the most popular car choice for locals. The city's campaign to "keep it weird" was evidenced everywhere—from the wacky street musicians on Pacific to the regular display of dreadlocks, body piercings, and tattoos on pedestrians.

It wasn't just the people who were different; the beaches maintained a vastly distinct personality from the ones I had grown to know in Southern California. Down south, they spanned and stretched—wide beaches that felt endless. In Santa Cruz, beaches were more like little enclaves between jagged rocks. But I quickly learned how to access all of them.

Just like sea turtles who could swim hundreds of miles in the ocean and always returned, year after year, to the exact spot they were born, I could have been plopped anywhere in this city on my bike and I could find my favorite beach spot.

I whizzed past the Boardwalk on my left. This had been one of Dad's selling points to get me to agree to the move, but after I had been a few times I lost interest in going. Tourists and families with kids too small for school flooded the pier, and it only got worse as schools started letting out for vacation. The Giant Dipper, a wooden roller coaster, whooshed and creaked as riders screamed, ascending down the first dramatic dip. Taking a right, I headed toward the water and then took another right onto Cliff, which spit me out onto the bike path at the ocean's edge.

I knew the curves on this trail better than any other road in the world. I sailed along past a smattering of ocean-view hotels; people throwing Frisbees on the grassy knoll in front of the Surfing Museum; and the huge, million-dollar beachfront houses until I hit a view of Seal Rock.

Some college couple was making out on the bench I usually occupied. Guess I wasn't the only one who appreciated the view.

I faked a hacking cough to ruin the mood. Their lips unlocked, and they turned toward me. I didn't budge. Sensing my refusal to leave, the guy gave his partner's hand a "let's go" squeeze, and they got up and made their way back up to the walking path.

The bench, the view, the beach were *mine*.

Out in the water on a lone, large rock, about a hundred seals all huddled together. This was my favorite time to watch them, when they were taking their afternoon siesta, tired from a morning of hunting and playing. Along with the seals came the threat of great white sharks. The surfers sometimes spotted them, and, once in a while, there would be an attack, most likely a shark mistaking a surfboard and its occupant for a seal; they have notoriously bad vision. Over the past two weeks I had wished on numerous occasions that a shark would accidentally mistake Andy's surfboard for a seal. I was never afraid of what lurked in the water. I used to swim as far out as I could. Mom taught me how to hold my breath and dive down deep.

It had been almost two years since I'd set foot in the ocean, but I was still constantly drawn to it, even though the thought of my body actually being in the water was utterly overwhelming. So instead, I'd watch from a distance, sometimes imagining myself swimming, sometimes pretending Mom was there, hidden among the waves. It was impossible to escape the water, especially living on the West Coast. When I thought about it, even my own body was more than 70 percent water.

Walking along the path was a little girl with pigtails holding her father's hand. I took out my black notebook and started one of my famous lists. My scientific brain was always trying to categorize and organize information.

This one was called *Resolutions*.

> *Study hard for my upcoming finals.*
> *Make more of an effort to hang out with the girls,*
> *even if I feel like being alone.*
> *Stay away from all guys.*
> *Try to hang out with Dad. (Do something nice for him.)*

Seemed simple enough. I flipped through the other pages of lists that included things like *What I'm Looking for in a College* and *Ways to Get Over Andy Dunn.* Some of the items were crossed off, if I had accomplished them, but others remained as a reminder of how little I ever seemed to get done, like the relentlessness of the waves that continually crashed along the shoreline.

Below me, serious beachgoers had staked their claim to prime sunning spots, the sand covered in a smattering of colorful umbrellas and towels. I didn't realize how much time had passed as I sat on my bench. Something about the salty air and sea breeze made it feel as though time were standing still, and yet, before I knew it, it was four o'clock. I could have stayed longer, but when I heard the clinking of collars and leashes, it was time to go.

As luck would have it, on the other side of my favorite bench was a makeshift dog park. I had inherited my mom's brown hair and hazel eyes and her propensity for freckles on her arms. I'd also inherited her fear of dogs—or, to use the more technical term, *cynophobia.* I guess my fear wasn't really in the genes but, as Mr. Sommers, my bio teacher, would say, a learned behavior: Mom was attacked by a pit bull when she was sixteen.

When I used to touch the big scar on her forearm, she would make a barking sound and simultaneously jolt her body, always scaring me just the right amount to keep me coming back for more.

Luckily, the leash law was only lifted for one hour in the morning and one hour in the evening. The dogs ran around spastically, and their owners followed with little colored plastic baggies, picking up dog poop.

A lanky guy in a UC Santa Cruz sweatshirt came jogging up to me.

"Excuse me, would you mind watching Corky for a minute? I have to use the restroom." Before I could say no, he went ahead and tied a red, fraying leash to my bench and trotted toward the public bathrooms. At the other end of the leash was what looked like a rat trying to pass for a dog. The dog looked up at me and whimpered. I stared back, petrified.

He kept sniffing my ankles even though I was shooing him away. I lifted both legs onto the bench.

"I hate dogs," I said to the creature by my feet, hoping he'd take pity on me and just leave me alone.

He only sniffed in response.

After what felt like a lifetime, the owner returned.

"Thanks so much," the man said, taking back the leash. "Corky's like my baby."

The man carried the dog down the path that led to the beach, and in a few minutes it was weaving in and out of the legs of a Great Dane. I brought my focus back to Seal Rock. The pinnipeds were stirring, some climbing over others, awakening them from their afternoon slumber. The seals dove headfirst into the water. Then they began barking, competing with the dogs' barking. Soon, seals were entering the water from all sides of the rock—headfirst, tail first, belly flopping, and haphazardly sliding into the water.

On the ride home I thought about my resolutions. Every change started with one step. Tonight, I'd start with Dad. I'd do something nice for him. Even though he was busy with work, I hadn't exactly made much of an effort either. Pumping up the hill to our home in Seabright, I decided that tonight I'd surprise him with dinner. I stopped by our corner store and, using my ATM card, grabbed a baguette and all the fixings for chicken salad. If worse came to worst, we could enjoy peanut butter and jelly sandwiches together. It didn't matter what we ate—as long as we had some time together. We could really talk; I could even tell him how depressed I'd been lately.

At home, I grabbed the mail and locked my bike to the fence out front. The neighbor's dog, a huge bullmastiff, barked at the sound of the rattling lock. It always got my adrenaline rushing. The neighbor kept that dog fenced in outside all the time, and I was convinced that if it ever got out, it was coming straight for me, the Bike Chain Lady.

Calla lilies lined our driveway and reminded me of that Diego Rivera painting with the woman holding a huge bundle in her arms, like she was hugging them. I made a mental note to pick some and put them in a vase as a centerpiece for our dinner tonight.

We lived on the top story of a duplex, but the unit below us was usually empty. It was owned by people who lived in San Anselmo and used this home as their "vacation" home. Once in a while they'd come down for a weekend in the summer, so we rarely saw them.

I dumped my stuff in my room and went straight to the kitchen to get to work on my father-daughter bonding meal, preparing the chicken and washing the lettuce. I had all of the garlic cloves peeled and pressed for the garlic bread when Dad walked in the door. For once, he wasn't on the phone.

"Hey!" I said, full of optimism and excitement.

"Smells funny in here," Dad said.

"It's the garlic." I pointed to my large plate of crushed garlic that had occupied the last thirty minutes of my life.

"What's it for?"

"For us. Dinner. I thought I'd make us some food," I said.

Dad looked around the kitchen, from the salad soaking in the colander to the chicken roasting in the oven.

"Iris…"

This wasn't good.

Dad couldn't even make eye contact with me. "I'm so sorry, but

I have plans tonight."

"Work meeting?" I asked. It was the usual reason he was never around at dinner. "Actually, more like...a date," Dad said casually.

"A date?"

He nodded.

The waters swiftly rose to their absolute breaking point. Why was this driving me nuts? Mom had been dead for almost two years. I should be okay with this. I should want my dad to be happy...to move on if he was ready.

But I wasn't.

He had been so busy over the past year and a half working on this job promotion, we never did anything together anymore—and then the first free moment he has he chooses to spend with a complete stranger?

"Who is she?"

"Her name is Janet. She works at the plant. She helps with the bookkeeping. She's new. They hired her a few months ago, and we just hit it off. It wasn't even really my idea," he continued defensively. "The guys at work...they just think it's time."

I held back tears with all my might. But one escaped. I tried to brush it away before he could notice.

In my head was a running monologue of insults to sling at my dad—*deadbeat, jerk*—but none of them left my lips. I just stood there, silent.

I must've looked utterly pathetic because Dad said, "You know, I'll cancel. Let me just call Janet."

But by the time the words came out of his mouth, I wasn't sad anymore. I was angry—angry that he was making time for this Janet but didn't have a second for me. Angry that he hadn't even brought up the meeting at school, like I was just supposed to pretend it didn't happen. And, most of all, I was angry that he didn't realize just how angry I was.

"Forget it," I said. "I'll invite the girls over instead." Little did he know they weren't really *my* girls—at least not at the moment. I had blown off meeting them on Pacific this afternoon, and I had ignored all subsequent e-mails and texts. There had been a lot of them to ignore.

"Are you sure?" he asked, eager that he might actually have an out.

"Yeah, positive."

I had no intention of inviting the girls over. The second he walked out that door smelling of awful cologne and hair gel, I dumped the food into the trash and went to my room.

I grabbed the hammer from my bedside drawer and went straight to my closet, bearing down on an unaltered section of the wall. I pounded and pounded as the plaster gathered at my feet. When my fingers began cramping from my tight grip, I released the hammer and caught my breath.

Instantly, I felt a bit better. I rearranged my clothing to cover up any evidence of my anger.

three

My performance on this morning's English final would seal my summer fate. But instead of studying, I had spent the majority of the weekend simply staring at my various textbooks. I had completely memorized the covers: the rendering of the shiny compass on my math book, the portrait of Shakespeare on my book of grammar, and the broad-shouldered matador on my Spanish book—but the books themselves all had remained closed.

I barely managed to wade through history, Spanish 3, and precalculus. I did okay with history—maybe a B—and I'd be lucky if I got a C-plus in Spanish and math, but at least I knew I passed. I should have been studying more, but everything seemed to distract me. The weekend was kind of a wash. Between marathon music-listening sessions, the next-door neighbor's dog barking at all hours of the night, and Dad's cell going off every five minutes (he had that annoyingly loud rumba ring), I had found it difficult to concentrate. Early in the week my computer had pinged at full throttle; the girls were smothering me with instant messages, wondering where I was and why I wasn't returning any of their phone calls and why in the world Mr. Cagle had wanted to meet with me.

Finally, when the last day of my junior year of high school arrived,

I was determined to get to school on time. While Dad was taking a shower, I filled my Monterey Bay Aquarium souvenir to-go cup with whatever was left in the coffeemaker. I even left the house and was on my bike fifteen minutes earlier than normal.

Outside, the morning mist reminded me of a Carl Sandberg poem I'd memorized in middle school when I was living in Los Angeles—"The fog comes/on little cat feet"—but in Santa Cruz it was more like tiger paws, thick and dewy until the mid-morning sun burned through the haze.

As I made my way up Water Street, I kept replaying the past week in my head: the scene in Mr. Cagle's office, struggling through all those finals, exams that had once come easily to me, when I had the focus and determination to actually sit down and study. Was this how it was going to be from now on? It felt as though I were stuck in a long tunnel with no end in sight. My only solace was thinking about summer break—time I could spend away from school—and then, looking further to the end of next year, when I would be out of high school and heading to college. Away from Dad. Away from Andy. Away from Santa Cruz. It would be a completely fresh start.

Just then I hit a large crack in the sidewalk, and a loud popping sound came from my back tire, startling me out of my daydream. My handlebars swiveled out of control. Luckily, there were no cars coming as I swerved in and out of the bike lane before hitting the curb and falling over, right next to a bus stop where some Santa Cruz High kids were waiting.

I wanted to have the perfect, witty thing to say to them as I heaved myself up off the concrete, but instead, keeping my eyes down, I surveyed my bike and assessed the damage.

Handlebars: busted.

Left leg: bloodied.

Tire and ego: deflated.

"Are you okay?" asked a boy who might've been a freshman.

Too shaken from the fall to speak, I just nodded my head. My fingers trembled as I picked up my bike.

There was no way I was getting to school on this mess of metal. After locking the bike to a nearby parking meter, I waited for the bus with the other students, thankful that I'd gotten an early start; I could still make it to my final on time.

When I finally arrived at school, I still had a few minutes to spare. I had planned on finding a seat in the gymnasium-turned-exam-room, so I could really focus, whip out my grammar studies book, and start cramming.

But the sight of Ashley and Sierra talking and laughing outside the gym distracted me. Maybe that shopping trip to San Francisco would do me some good. I thought about telling them about my fall; I could probably have used some comforting words before walking into this final. But when I got to them, they stopped laughing and seemed like they were trying to avoid eye contact with each other.

"Is this a bad time?" I asked. Not knowing what else to say and feeling, once again, like the new girl, I reached down to grasp my left knee, which was still throbbing.

"Are you okay?" asked Ashley.

"Yeah, what happened to you? You look stressed out," said Sierra.

I decided just then that I didn't want to get into the embarrassing details of my accident. "It's finals week; I'm sure I'm not the only one," I said.

Sierra looked at Ashley and rolled her eyes. Maybe now wasn't the right time for my sarcasm.

"So, last day," I said, trying to feign optimism.

"Yup," said Ashley, unusually quiet.

We stood there awkwardly. Why did things feel so weird?

Luckily, buggy-eyed Lydia Cordova sidled up to us. She was always overly enthusiastic about everything, which Ashley and I used to make fun of when we were alone.

"Can you believe it!" she squealed. "It's the last day of school!" Sierra and Ashley giggled, affirming Lydia's enthusiasm. I had said the exact same thing not thirty seconds ago and had been met by silence.

"I am so excited you guys conference-called me last night! I can't wait to go shopping in San Francisco this weekend! It's gonna be so much fun! Ashley, please thank your mom for me. And I've never stayed at a hotel as nice as the Fairmont before!"

And then it all clicked—I'd been ousted from my spot in the Volvo and replaced by Lydia.

Even though I knew my own recent isolation was responsible for being left out, it still stung.

There was nothing I could say, so I walked away, toward my final.

"Iris, wait!" shouted Ashley. I thought about turning around and going back to talk with them about the situation, like adults. But then Sierra said, purposely loud enough for me to hear, "It's not like she even *wants* to hang out with us anyways."

So I kept walking.

✻

I entered the gym, where all of Mrs. Schneider's five English classes were taking the same final. I picked a seat in the back and didn't even bother to open up my book. I was seething. I needed some sort of release. If I didn't care about what other people thought about my sanity, I'd have let out a guttural scream. I'd give anything to be in my closet, hammer in hand. I looked down at my knee. Still bloody. Students filed in, some with confidence in their eyes that said they had spent the weekend actually studying.

Hoodie Boy, part of the bad-boy crew who had lobbed a paper bag at Ashley's head the week before, took a seat next to me. If he was planning on cheating off my exam, he picked the wrong person.

Then Andy and that soon-to-be sophomore trotted in together, holding hands. What was she even doing in the gym anyway? She was in ninth grade. And even if she were in accelerated English, she wouldn't be in our English class. She took a seat on his lap and ran her fingers through his hair.

"There is a time and a place, Mr. Dunn," Mrs. Schneider said to him.

I thought the nauseating scene was over and his new "friend" would take her cue and flee the premises, but instead she took him by the hand, led him out of the gym, and started making out with him in the doorway. At one point, I thought I could see Andy's eyes open and look straight at me, but then they closed again, and the two of them continued their suck fest.

I felt sick to my stomach.

Five more minutes to spare. The walls of the gymnasium felt as though they were closing in on me. The whole world was closing in on me.

I pulled out my black journal and opened to an empty page. Time for a new list.

"PEOPLE I WANT TO BASH WITH MY HAMMER," I wrote in big block letters.

If I could write it out on paper, maybe I'd get some sort of release from the pain.

Then I began to list them:

Andy (and his stupid girlfriend)
Sierra
Ashley
Lydia
Dad

And just when I thought I was done, I caught Mrs. Schneider filing her long fingernails while glaring at the clock, waiting to see who she would be able to give tardy slips to in another minute. She lived to torture us. So I started a new list.

PEOPLE I WANT TO KILL
Mrs. Schneider

Air filled my lungs at a normal pace. I had just saved myself from doing something extremely stupid, like hurling a desk across the gymnasium or throwing a book at Andy's head.

I closed the journal and placed it in my lap, wanting to keep the list close to me, reminding me how good it felt to get the rage out.

The bell rang, everyone took their seats, and the English exam began.

I scanned the eight pages of questions, and I felt I actually had a chance of passing this final. There wasn't nearly as much sentence graphing as Mrs. Schneider had threatened. Maybe this day could do a one-eighty.

Mrs. Schneider paced the room with both hands behind her back like a prison guard. I tried to focus on the task at hand, but before

I knew it, she was hovering over me like a blimp, casting a shadow on my paper.

"Iris Moody?"

I looked up. Her steely blue eyes met mine. I was on a roll, picking out all of the prepositions in a sentence, and now she'd gone and disrupted my rhythm.

"What's that in your lap?" she asked.

I looked down. My black book.

A few students turned around to check out what was going on. Blood rushed to my cheeks.

"Pass me the book," Schneider commanded.

I hesitated.

"Cheating is grounds for expulsion," she said, loud enough that it seemed most students shifted in their seats to watch the drama unfolding behind them. Schneider took the book off my lap and began flipping through my lists of my innermost personal thoughts.

"Do you mind?" I asked. What right did she have to look through something so intimate? It should have been fairly obvious to her that it wasn't filled with English exam answers.

She flipped though the pages and paused at my most recent entry. Why did I have to write the title in block letters? I knew she had arrived at her own name when her expression suddenly registered the shock of someone who has been slapped across the face.

"Interesting." She looked at me.

"I told you I wasn't cheating," was all I could think of to say to her.

"I think you'll find this is worse. Much, much worse. Pack up your things and come with me."

I quickly rose to my feet and lunged for the book. It was mine. She had no right to be looking at it, but she held on tight. It was an intense game of tug of war. Who knew Schneider had so much strength? I wasn't gaining any ground by pulling the book, so I tried a new strategy and pushed the book forward with all of my strength, accidentally throwing Mrs. Schneider off balance. The book was back in my possession, but the force of my jostling had sent her flying backward and down to the ground. I hadn't meant to push her. I just wanted my book back. This was merely physics at work.

Another teacher proctoring the exam rushed to her aid and helped her up.

Schneider snatched my notebook and grabbed my unfinished English final from my desk, and, as she instructed, I packed my pen and water bottle in my backpack. I slid the loop of my bike helmet around my wrist, and it clanked against each desk I passed as I followed Schneider toward the exit door of the gym.

Turning to the other proctor, Schneider whispered, "I'll be right back."

As I was being escorted out of the building, I accidentally happened on Andy's once-familiar blue eyes. They showed no sign of compassion or empathy. In that moment, I let him go forever.

✿

Things went quickly from bad to worse. I was turned over to campus security—a large balding man who stood next to me outside the gym, speaking into his walkie-talkie.

"I have the suspect in custody," he answered when the voice of Mr. Cagle, on the other end of the contraption, asked, "Where's Ms. Moody now?"

Joe (as his nametag indicated) seemed to be living out his fantasies of feeling very important.

We stood there for a long time. So long, in fact, that some speedy exam takers handed in their finals and were exiting the gym when the cops finally did show up.

"Seriously? The police?" I questioned Joe, confused at the sight of the man and woman in uniform.

"Hit list. Death threat. You caused a big stir in there," said Joe, adjusting his security belt.

No one was supposed to read that list. Those were my private thoughts. But none of that seemed to matter now.

Mr. Cagle emerged from wherever he was to shake both officers' hands. I stood next to Joe and watched them speak, and then Mr. Cagle entered the gym and produced Mrs. Schneider, who had to come out presumably to give them a statement. She presented my black book and handed it over to the police officers, who took a look at the inciting page, nodded, and placed my journal in a large Ziploc bag.

They then approached me.

"Iris Moody," said the woman, "you are under arrest for violating California Penal Code Section 422."

I had officially become a criminal.

❀

We used to play a game at recess in elementary school. The boys would be the captors and run around chasing the girls. I know—totally chauvinistic. When they caught us, they'd grab our wrists tightly and hold them behind our backs as they led us to the sandbox jail.

Being cuffed by real officers on my high school campus was much more painful than my memory of make-believe.

"Let's go," said the male cop as he gently nudged me on the shoulder, urging me to walk as though I were a horse tethered to a wagon. Ashley happened to be walking by as they led me to the car. Her mouth was agape. Her eyes said, "Who are you?"

Mine answered back, "I don't know."

※

I'm not saying that jail is the kind of place I *ever* want to be again, but I will say that there was something kind of nice about sitting with my thoughts for six hours (yes, it took that long for them to reach my dad). After going through the motions—mug shot, emptying out my pockets, removing my gold necklace, and giving them all of my personal information—I was led to an empty cell and tried to take as much pleasure as I could from the silence. No exams, no Andy, no catty friends, no Dad.

My meditative bliss eventually wore off, and, after a crappy meal consisting of mushy beans, corn, and turkey, a guard came to my cell.

"Moody, it's time to go."

I followed the guard to the registration officer from earlier; she handed me a sealed envelope containing my gold necklace and pocket contents.

"Dad knows best. Just remember that," she offered.

Not my dad, I wanted to say, but I just nodded and took my things. Dad was talking to the female officer as I slowly approached them.

"She's a good kid," he was saying. "I just don't understand how something like this could have happened."

"Make sure you both show up to her court date. Judges like to see that incarcerated teens have family support."

Great. *Incarcerated teen.* My new label.

Dad and I walked to the car in silence. I had to break the tension.

"Dad." It came out quieter than I had intended.

When he turned to face me, he didn't even make eye contact and instead looked beyond me to the cars in the lot.

"What in the world did you do?" he asked.

"Nothing. I mean, I was pissed off. I just wrote down—"

He interrupted me. "I had to walk out on a quarterly meeting with corporate. Do you know how embarrassing that was? How it could affect my promotion? I had to meet the cops at our house. They tore the place apart!"

"My stuff?" I could feel the blood rush to my cheeks as I thought of strangers looking through my belongings.

"Our stuff, but yeah, mostly yours. They confiscated your computer. And took some journals."

My old diaries had been lined up in chronological order under the bed.

"They read them?" I asked, panicked at the thought of more of my private thoughts becoming public.

We had reached our car.

"Well, I don't think they plan on using them as doorstops," said Dad.

"That's bull—" I began.

"Watch your language," Dad snapped. He unlocked the door, then got into the car and slammed the door shut. I sat in the backseat, as I had in the police car.

After staring at the steering wheel for what seemed like ages, he lifted his head and finally spoke. "What's gotten into you lately, Iris? First the grades. Now death threats and physical assault?"

I felt the tears well up in the corners of my eyes. I tried to form my thoughts into articulate sentences before speaking. I was about to tell him everything—lay it all on the line: how the breakup affected me, how I'd been feeling so isolated and depressed. How it felt as though no one wanted to hear anything negative come out of me so I just kept it all inside. But before I could get the words out, Dad spoke again.

"I don't have time for this, Iris. Things are happening for me at work. Big things. I'm up for that promotion. I just really need to focus right now."

I felt so stupid for assuming I was going to have a heart-to-heart with a man who was so self-consumed he didn't possess the ability to see the person sitting two feet away from him. Fighting a burning feeling inside my throat, I said the words he wanted to hear.

"I'm sorry. It won't happen again."

At home, we didn't say anything to each other for the rest of the evening, each of us holed up in our respective ends of the house.

☼

By morning, the stress from the day before had gathered between my shoulders and at the base of my neck. On the table was a note from Dad, scribbled on a paper towel: *Making up for lost time at work. Stay out of trouble.*

I made a fresh pot of coffee, poured myself a bowl of cereal, and sat at the kitchen table. At least with my computer confiscated, I didn't have to deal with any of the girls' IMs. And Dad had stripped me of all cell phone privileges, so I could avoid their texts as well. God knows what rumors had circulated about me yesterday. The only thing I had going for me was that school was out for the summer—so if anyone wanted to talk about me, they'd have to do so off campus.

When the house phone started ringing, I thought it best to ignore it and just let the machine pick up.

"Iris, this is Mrs. Harrison. This is a very uncomfortable call for me to make because I know how much Conor and Hunter love you, but in light of recent events, I'm going to have to cancel my babysitting request for this summer."

In the background, I could hear Conor calling my name before Mrs. Harrison hung up.

My stomach cramped up. It was one thing to let myself down, but now I'd disappointed these two boys.

I wondered how she had gotten wind of my situation and then remembered that the whole reason I had gotten the job in the first place was because my PE teacher, Coach Lutz, knew Mrs. Harrison because they lived on the same street. He must have called her as soon as word got out at school.

My dream summer was turning into anything but.

four

Dad thought he was punishing me by grounding me for an entire week. Little did he know the last thing I wanted to do was interact with anyone. I was happy to stay on the couch, consume mass quantities of the free juice that he brought home (beet-carrot-apple was my favorite), watch my nature shows, and listen to my music. My two current favorite shows were *The Underwater World* and *Abe Lives with Apes*. Living in the ocean, living in the jungle—I'd take either of those habitats over my own.

About a week after *the incident*, I went back to the police station to collect my confiscated computer and journals. Dad had picked up my totaled bike and had given me his to borrow, but it was a guy's bike, which meant that sitting on it for long periods of time became quite uncomfortable because the saddle was too narrow.

"Did you find lots of incriminating evidence?" I asked the officer who handed my laptop back to me.

"You'll find out soon enough," she said, referring to my upcoming court date.

I was appointed a lawyer (Nathaniel Spencer), and Dad gave me my cell phone back and let me leave the house only to meet with Mr. Spencer to discuss my case. Mr. Spencer said the best we could do was defend my actions and hope for the best. He said it all depended upon who the judge was the day of my trial and what kind of mood he or she was in.

Great.

The police must have been sorely disappointed by my hard drive. No bomb-making recipes, no plans to follow through on my threats. Just a lot of bookmarked nature websites and a collection of e-mails from Ashley wondering what in the world was going on, each subsequent e-mail decreasing in friendliness. In her first e-mail sent after my arrest, she sympathetically checked in about what she had heard at school. In the second, she mentioned she'd be out of town (San Francisco) and that I should call her when she got back. By the third e-mail she laid out everything that bugged her about me and wrote that maybe we should take the summer off as friends. I had managed to completely alienate my closest friend just by being this version of myself. How could I blame her for criticizing me?

But I was still too hurt to respond, and I convinced myself that I didn't need her anyway.

The television would become my new best friend.

But then, toward the end of the week, I tortured myself by going online and looking at photos of the girls in San Francisco. There was stupid Lydia Cordova posing with my friends on the Golden Gate Bridge, in front of Coit Tower, and in Golden Gate Park.

I had been replaced.

✿

Dad was standing in the kitchen hovering next to the coffee machine on the day of my trial. "So what are you doing with yourself today?" Dad acted like he had genuinely forgotten.

"I have my trial this afternoon, remember? You're supposed to be there."

Dad's big promotion was coming up soon. I figured once he got it, things would calm down again. He'd be in his big new office. Making more money. I only had to deal with this distracted Dad for twenty-one more days.

"Yeah, kid." His eyes darted back and forth, searching his porous memory for anything to trigger this promise he'd made to be at my trial.

"You *have* to be there," I said.

"What time?" he asked.

"Two-thirty," I lied, hoping that faking an earlier start time would get him there by three.

I watched as he entered *be at trial* into his phone calendar. Sometimes I wanted to grab his phone and hurl it into the ocean.

"You have to put it into your phone to remember?"

"Iris, you know how busy things are for me right now. I can't keep it all straight. If it's not in my phone, it doesn't exist."

I poured myself the last of the coffee.

"Iris, no more coffee."

I rolled my eyes.

"Two-thirty at the courthouse," I said as Dad dashed out the door to work.

I took a seat and gave myself a moment to breathe. I'd been dreading this day for two weeks, but at the same time, I was looking forward to getting it over with. I just wanted to fast-forward through time to my life post-sentencing—whatever my fate may be.

I had only one outfit appropriate to wear in court—the dress I'd worn to my mother's funeral. Even though it was two years old, it still fit; the rayon stretched as my body grew. When I first bought the dress in a secondhand store on Melrose Avenue in Hollywood, I imagined all of the fun parties I'd get to wear it to. It was stylish and graceful but also rebellious, with an aquamarine sheen shimmering underneath the black tulle.

When my mom died, it was the only dress I owned elegant enough to wear to a funeral, and after that it became my depression dress. If I was wearing it, things were bad. I wore it to Mom's memorial a year after her death, I wore it the day we moved to Santa Cruz, and now I was wearing it to receive my court sentencing.

Dad had cleaned out our home in Topanga pretty quickly and thoroughly after Mom died. Her style wasn't simpatico with mine, so I let go of a lot of her stuff—Dad encouraged its rapid elimination. But I did keep a bunch of her jewelry, which I housed in a keepsake box at the back of my underwear drawer. I riffled through my meager collection and put on two small gold hoop earrings and remembered what it was like to be close to my mom, who always smelled of a mix of citrus and cinnamon.

✼

I'm not a bad person. I tried to talk myself up as I parked and locked my bike in front of the courthouse. My heart raced.

The phrase got stuck in my head like the chorus of a catchy song.

Even though I wanted to run in the opposite direction, I forced my body forward up the courthouse steps. Mr. Spencer was waiting for me in the shade of a cypress tree, finishing a sandwich. A piece of bologna fell out of the side of his mouth. He wiped his hands on his pants and extended his arm to shake my hand. Now there was a smear of mustard across his pant leg. This was the mess of a guy who was responsible for my future? I reluctantly reached out my hand.

He might have been a disaster, but at least he was willing to help me out.

For a moment, I felt the tears well up in my eyes. I couldn't start crying. Not now. If I started, I didn't know that I would be able to stop. At least when Dad arrived, I could look to him for support if things got rough in there.

"Are you ready?" Mr. Spencer asked.

I shrugged. I didn't think anyone could ever really be ready for something like this.

"One sec," I said, pulling out my phone. I texted Dad: *Are you almost here?*

There was no response. I needed him to show up. Maybe he was already inside.

My lawyer led me up the concrete stairs and held the door open for me. Inside, we placed all metal objects—our keys, change, and cell phones—in a plastic container and walked through the metal detector. I followed him down a long hallway and into the courtroom, where I was about to learn my fate.

Court was already in session when we entered.

The room felt suffocating, the heat oppressive as bodies crammed together on the benches in the back, a combination of kids and their lawyers. The city hadn't invested in air-conditioning. Voices reverberated throughout the room. Mr. Spencer and I took our places on a bench alongside a few other people, and I scanned the room for Dad.

Still not here.

I checked the wall clock. He was officially late for the fake time I had given him, but not yet late for my actual court time.

A long-haired teenager sat next to his lawyer at a table across from the judge, who was surprisingly younger than I imagined she would be and, if not for the whole baggy robe, looked like a relatively nice person. Her hair was so curly, it looked like a wig. She was wearing a lace collar underneath her judge's robe. I wondered if she was considered a fashionista among her peers.

"Scott Haydon, how do you plead?"

The boy looked at his lawyer.

"Not guilty," the boy said with a slight smirk. The lawyer looked disappointed.

"Let's take a look at your paperwork." The judge riffled through a file. "Mr. Haydon, you are aware that vandalism is a crime you've committed not once, not twice, but three times."

"Yes, Your Honor." Scott Haydon knew how to address her. He'd obviously been through this process before.

"And you do realize that the fine people of Santa Cruz are the ones who have to pay to clean up the messes you've been leaving around town."

"Uh-huh."

"Uh-huh, Your Honor," she corrected.

I looked over at Mr. Spencer. He was shaking his head.

"What's wrong?" I whispered.

"She's in a bad mood. It doesn't bode well for us."

I knew there was no real *us*. *I* was the only one she was targeting. Nothing worse than the judge in charge of your fate being cranky.

The judge continued, "What I see here is a boy—even though you probably think you're a man—perhaps with some artistic talent. But all the talent in the world doesn't give you the right to break the law, Mr. Haydon. City walls are not your canvas." She paused, waiting for his response.

"Yeah, but they don't sell blank walls at the local art store, *Your Honor.*"

A few people in the room laughed.

"Is this some kind of a joke to you?" asked the judge.

His lawyer whispered something in his ear, which made him quickly lean into the microphone in front of him and say, "Sorry, Your Honor."

The judge continued, "This court has given you multiple chances to get your act together, and yet here you are again in the same place you were four months ago and two months before that. We are tired of spending money on you, Mr. Haydon. Perhaps a little time in juvenile hall will set you straight once and for all. My ruling is twenty-eight days in a detention center, and then we can revisit regarding parole."

She hit her gavel on the table, announcing the case's conclusion.

The boy's smirk disappeared, and he now looked broken, like this wasn't the result he was expecting. His mother and father made their way toward him. His dad put his hand on his shoulder, and his mom cried and hugged him.

This was his fate even with the "parental support" that was apparently so important. Dad still hadn't arrived. What would my fate be? Would I end up in jail, too? My face flushed, and I urgently needed to go to the bathroom.

"Case Number 4758392," said the bailiff.

Mr. Spencer tapped me on the shoulder. "That's you."

My bladder would have to wait.

The bailiff continued: "The State versus Iris Moody."

I followed my lawyer to the table, had a seat, and awaited my punishment.

The judge spread open my file in front of her. It was visibly slimmer than Scott Haydon's. This had to be a good thing.

"Ms. Moody, how do you plead?"

"Guilty." It was the first time I'd said the word out loud. Tears welled up again, and my nose started to tingle. If only Dad were here, just maybe I could pull it together. *Act like an adult for once*, a voice inside said.

I scanned the room. All eyes were on me. Dad was nowhere to be seen, and I couldn't hold it in anymore. I started to sob out of control, as though the entire Pacific Ocean swelled from within.

My lawyer looked panicked; he didn't know what to do with me. The bailiff walked over with a big box of tissues and placed it in front of me. I took one and brought it to my face.

"I can see this has deeply affected you," said the judge. "But dramatic blubbering is not going to change the way I handle things today."

This shut me up. Not because I had been crying to get sympathy but because now I was terrified of what was about to come out of her mouth.

"Death threats, even in a moment of rage, are not something we take lightly here. But since this is your first offense, and I hope your last, I am sentencing you to one hundred and twenty hours of community service. And to make sure you really get to the root of what's making you so angry, you'll need to see a state-certified therapist until I deem otherwise." She whacked her gavel on the table.

It was over. Before I knew what was happening, I was following Mr. Spencer out of the room, and another nervous girl and her lawyer were replacing us at the table.

"Well, that went well," Mr. Spencer said.

"Is one hundred and twenty hours good?" It sounded like a lot, but what did I know? Maybe two thousand was the norm.

"She's a tough judge. Wasn't supposed to be her today, but Judge

Chen was out sick. Six weeks isn't so bad…"

Six weeks? I quickly started doing the math in my head: four hours a day, twenty hours a week. Oh my God. It was six weeks.

"But that's my whole summer!"

"Could have been worse."

I didn't share Mr. Spencer's perspective. Not only had I lost my job, but now the remainder of my summer would be spent dealing with community service, therapists, and summer school. If the judge thought that this whole "plan" would make me less angry, she was sorely mistaken.

"What do we do next?" I asked.

"We can just step into my office, and the city will fax over the community service options. The good news is you'll get a list to choose from, so you can pick what interests you."

"What kinds of things do they have on there?"

"Well, the cream of the crop is dog rehabilitation, but it's always the first to go, especially over the summer—I'm sorry to say you don't have a chance of getting that assignment."

I didn't bother to share my severe aversion to dogs with Mr. Spencer.

"There's trash pickup, and things like city beautification, which includes gardening and painting over graffiti."

I imagined myself scrubbing Scott Haydon's art off the walls and his friends walking by and whispering, like they were out to get revenge on the person who erased his creations. I would not be choosing graffiti cleanup.

As we left the courthouse, I could see Dad running at a full sprint to meet us on the stairs. He couldn't talk when he reached us; he was too out of breath. He put his hands on his knees and dramatically heaved his chest in and out.

"Did I make it?" he asked.

"Nope," I said and looked to Mr. Spencer, hoping he'd take over condemning my dad for missing my court time. But Mr. Spencer just reached out his hand to shake Dad's and left it to me to do the talking.

"I can't even believe you," I said, furious.

"I'm so sorry, Iris. It was supposed to be a quick check-in about the budget, but then someone whipped out a spreadsheet, and next thing I knew, we were doing an annual overview."

"Why didn't you just leave? Why didn't you just tell them you had somewhere else to be?"

"I couldn't do that, Iris. With the promotion coming up, every action counts."

There was no use even engaging him in conversation. It was clear that, once again, he had chosen work over me.

"What can I do to help?" he asked Mr. Spencer.

"We were just heading over to my office to choose a community service assignment," said Mr. Spencer.

"How many hours did you get?" asked my dad.

"All summer," I said.

"I'll walk you guys over there," said Dad.

"Don't bother."

"Iris." Dad put his hand on my shoulder.

"I've made it this far on my own, Dad. The hard part is over. You can go back to work. I'll see you later."

I headed toward Mr. Spencer's office, and my lawyer, taking my lead, followed me down the honey locust–lined street and around the corner to an old brick building. Dad set off for the parking lot.

When we arrived at his office, I had a seat in front of Mr. Spencer's scattered desk.

"Ah! The fax is already here. Let's take a look." He began scanning the paper and muttering to himself. Empty candy wrappers covered his desk, along with piles upon piles of paper. I didn't understand how he got anything done in all that mess.

"Just like I thought, most of the slots have already been filled. Lots of teens postpone their hours until summer. Looks like it's either garbage collection or graffiti cleanup."

"Garbage pickup, please, Mr. Spencer."

"Great. I'll process this tonight, and you'll probably start your stint next week. Good luck to you, Iris."

He shook my hand. I hoped I would never have to see him again.

✿

At home, I gathered the envelopes from our mailbox. We never received anything fun in the mail—just bills and junk mail. The one piece of mail that I would be excited about next year would be a college acceptance letter.

Closing the metal lid of the mailbox triggered the neighbor's dog, who basically tried to attack me through the fence, lunging and thrashing, affirming my fear of these supposedly domesticated animals.

Inside, inspired by a nature show on the brown bear's hibernation patterns, I fell into a deep sleep.

Passed out on the couch, I dreamed of gavels and judges and jails. Keys clanged, and Mr. Spencer shoved papers to sign in my face. Amid the courthouse chaos, my mother sat still in a corner, watching me. She opened her arms, and I ran toward her, ready for a deep embrace, but when I reached her she disappeared, and I was left alone.

The house phone rang, jarring me awake. The machine beeped, and I heard Mr. Spencer's gravelly voice.

"Heya, Iris. Mr. Spencer here. Listen, I've got great news!"

Finally, someone with something good to report.

"There was an opening at Ruff Rehabilitation—the dog community service position I was telling you about that everyone wants. And guess what? I snagged it for you. Be cliffside at Natural Bridges Monday by one o'clock. You can thank me later."

five

Apparently my time in court had been more exhausting than I had realized—it was way past noon when I finally opened my eyes. Luckily summer school didn't start until the next week.

Was it all a dream, or had I really been assigned to community service work involving dogs? I forced myself out of bed and listened to Mr. Spencer's chipper voice on the machine again. To my major disappointment, it wasn't all a bad dream.

It was my reality.

There was hardly any coffee left in the pot (it was as though Dad were trying to punish me by finishing it all himself). I grabbed a pair of dirty jeans off the floor and threw on a sweatshirt. The dogs wouldn't care about my appearance. If I could just explain to whomever was in charge that I was absolutely the wrong person for this job, maybe they'd let me do office work or something in order to fulfill my community service requirement.

At Zachary's, my favorite breakfast spot on Pacific Avenue, I ordered their largest to-go cup of coffee. Even though the brew was better at Pergolesi, there was no way I was going to risk running into Ashley there. So much for my summer of free coffee.

I had the fortunate talent of being able to ride a bike one-handed so that my other hand could be free to swat at mosquitoes, gesticulate at bad drivers, or drink a cup of coffee.

Picking up speed down toward Ocean Avenue, I took a right, pedaling fast past families of bikers on vacation.

"Slow down!" a protective dad yelled.

But this was *my* bike lane. I couldn't help but count the number of dogs I passed as I zoomed by. Ten, eleven, twelve...ugh. They were everywhere. *Ubiquitous*, as Mrs. Schneider would say. (There were a few things I learned in school that year; for some reason, vocab stuck.)

When I got to Natural Bridges State Beach, I locked my bike to a stop sign post and raced full speed ahead to the community center. Why couldn't this gig have been somewhere private where we wouldn't be susceptible to public scrutiny? Would everyone who walked past know we were convicts? Or would they just think we were training our pets? If they made us wear fluorescent orange uniforms like those guys who picked up trash on the side of the road I would be so mortified. My palms started to sweat when I saw a circle of teens holding leashes attached to various-sized dogs. I recognized only one of the figures, standing there with a German shepherd. It was Hoodie Boy from school—part of that group that was always getting into trouble. I had now sunk to his level. His sweatshirt, as usual, was still drawn tightly around his face. I was so embarrassed to know someone there.

I slowed down my frantic pace, now trying to take as long as possible to avoid having to participate.

"You must be Iris!" a guy shouted from across the grass. "Come on over!" He waved me toward him. Everyone stared. I suddenly became self-conscious about everything: my hair, my walk, my choice of clothing. Were my arms swinging too much? Too little? I put my head down so my hair covered my face. I didn't want anyone to be able to "read me."

"We were just getting acquainted. I'm Kevin." He put his hand out. I had no choice but to shake it.

Kevin was not what I expected a dog rehabilitator to look like. He resembled a surfer more than anything else: long blond hair, super-tanned physique.

"Since you're late…"

"It wasn't my fault," I lied, ready to make up some excuse about my dad losing my bike-lock key.

"Everyone got a chance to choose their dogs already," Kevin said.

"Hey, I didn't get a choice!" said a huge, towering boy in an oversized plaid jacket and baggy pants that made him look even bigger.

"Randy, you *did* have a choice," said Kevin.

"Yeah, between the Chihuahua and the peg leg. Lesser of two evils," said Randy.

At the end of Randy's red leash was the ugliest thing I've ever seen—even worse than the dog I'd had to watch at the beach a few weeks earlier. The Chihuahua's fur was tattered, and it had an exaggerated underbite.

A girl with wild hair laughed at Randy. "You two are like yin and yang."

They all laughed.

I took stock of my surroundings. Two girls. Two guys. And me. That made five of us suffering through the same summer stint. What had each of them done to land themselves here? And were they wondering the same about me?

"Let's go around and introduce ourselves," said Kevin.

"Again?" complained Hoodie Boy. It was the first time I had

actually heard him speak.

"I'm Kevin, your fearless leader. I'm here to help you train your dog. But more on that later. As you know, you all are now members of the most coveted community service gig out there. We like to keep the group small so you get a chance to really bond with your animal."

Was this guy for real? I'd rather bond with a snake…a slug…a tarantula.

"I'm Randy, and I hope I don't fall on my dog because it won't survive." The Chihuahua yapped away.

"Do you remember your dog's name?" asked Kevin.

"Tinkerbelle," he said. "This is so ridiculous."

At least I wasn't the only one who felt this way.

Next to Randy was a girl with a funky haircut: her brown hair long in front and short in back, with pink highlights. She wore a big army-green shirt that looked like it had gotten into a fight with a pair of scissors and lost. A quote on a patch sewn to her knee read, PROPERTY IS THEFT.

"I'm Talbot, and this dog here is Garrett. He's part Doberman, part retriever." The dog licked her face, and I could feel myself start to have a panic attack. "And *all* love."

"Shelley," said the quiet brunette. "Bruce," she added as she looked down at the bulldog licking itself at her feet.

Last but not least was Hoodie Boy. His legs were tangled up in his dog's leash. "The dog is named Persia. German shepherd, right?"

Kevin nodded.

"And I'm Oak and I really don't want to be here."

For some reason I was taken aback to learn that Hoodie Boy actually had a real name other than what the girls and I had been calling him for so long.

The girls. I wondered what Ashley and Sierra were doing at this very moment. I was jealous of their freedom to have a summer break.

"No one wants to be here," said Randy, as though reading my mind.

"I think it's fun!" said Talbot, leaning down to kiss her dog.

So gross.

The long silence made me fidgety. What were we supposed to do now?

"Hello?" said Talbot.

Was she talking to me?

"It's your turn," said Kevin, gesturing toward me.

Before I could get my name out, Hoodie Boy said, "That's Iris." I couldn't believe that he knew my name. Then I remembered that Kevin had called it out when I'd first arrived; also, word had probably spread about what I'd done at school. Most likely Oak had already shared my crime with the entire group.

"Yeah, I'm Iris, and I don't have a dog. Which is totally fine by me."

"Oh yes, you do," said Randy. "You have my sloppy seconds."

Everyone laughed but me.

"Let me run and get him," said Kevin, and he took off toward the community building. He emerged moments later, dog on leash.

"Iris, this is Roman. He is a pit bull."

My heart raced. The week before, I had watched a show called *World's Most Dangerous Pets*. And pit bulls were number one on the list, which, after what happened to my mom, didn't surprise me in the least. They were killing machines. And when they weren't killing people, surely they were *thinking* about killing them.

The compact brown dog on the other end of Kevin's leash looked like a bicep with legs and had an expression on his face like he was hungry. For flesh. Kevin extended the leash out toward me, but when I reached for it, my hands shook so badly I had to put them back at my side.

"Gimp!" said Randy. *The waters swelled inside.* I was ready to run away and do time in juvenile hall—anything was better than this.

"You could name-call," Kevin said to Randy, "or I could tell you Roman's story and maybe you'd have a bit more sympathy."

I wondered what in the world they were talking about—and then, as I scanned the eighty pounds of pure muscle in front of me, I realized that the dog I was so petrified of was missing his back left leg. The tan fur had grown over where the limb had been, and the muscles there moved and pulsed as though a phantom limb were attached.

So that was it.

I showed up late and got the worst possible dog available—the one no one else wanted. The dog that had lost some of its dog-ness. I was so mad I wanted to kick the dog in all three of its working legs, but I was too afraid it would respond by killing me, so I just left my sweaty hands at my side and listened to Kevin.

"Roman hasn't had an easy life. None of these dogs has. I know all their stories well, and as the dogs' official trainers, it's important that you learn their stories, too. If you can understand the dog you're working with, you'll be able to train it much more effectively."

Roman sat and scratched his ear with his one back leg. So weird looking.

"Roman was born on the streets and was picked up by an illegal dog-fighting ring."

"What's that?" asked Talbot, adjusting the small silver stud in her nose.

"The dogs fight each other, and people bet on it. My uncle used to do it with roosters," said Oak. He tugged both cords around his hood, and the fabric tightened against his face. I made it my mission to see his forehead before the summer was over.

"That's so mean," said Talbot, hugging her dog.

Kevin continued, "Essentially, people pay to see dogs tear each other apart. More often than not, both dogs wind up badly injured. Many die. And then there's the psychological ramifications. Roman here was in a fighting ring for a long time. He was a prizefighter, until he met his match. Another dog attacked him so severely it ruined his back leg, and his owner had no use for him. Animal rescue services found him wandering the streets. He had lost so much blood from his back leg, it had to be amputated. We traced him back to his owner, whose daughter told us Roman's story. Her dad is doing jail time now for animal abuse."

"Is that what all those scars are from? The fighting?" asked Shelley, still talking in practically a whisper.

I looked more closely at what she was referring to. All along Roman's fur were small lines, scars telling stories of his previous life. His body resembled dolphins I'd seen in the ocean who had been hit by boats or attacked by sharks, their rubbery skin covered in slash marks that would never heal. I did feel sorry for the dog, but at the same time, Kevin had just verified that he really was a trained killing machine. What business did I have training Roman? Was I, an incarcerated teen, so disposable that I could be used as an experiment in this killer-dog training process?

As though Kevin could read my thoughts, he added, "Just to let you know, Roman has been in training for a long time, Iris. There's nothing to be afraid of. We would never give you a dog who was dangerous."

"If he's all trained, then why is he still *here*?" asked Randy. I couldn't even see Tinkerbelle, who was hiding behind his massive legs.

"Well, he still needs work—it's a slow process to undo all the damage that's been done and have him gain our trust. Also, it's really hard to adopt out a three-legged dog. People want a dog that looks like…" Kevin paused, contemplating his word choice.

"A dog?" said Talbot.

"Exactly, but I think you'll find that Roman can do everything other dogs can do." Kevin handed the leash to me. "You ready for him?"

No. I wasn't ready to take charge of a recovering killer. I wouldn't ever be ready—but did I have a choice? I reached out my shaky arm to Kevin. As soon as I made contact with the leash, Roman ran over to me and sniffed my feet. I kicked them up and toward his nose to shoo him away. He growled, and my fingers automatically released the leash.

The dog took off across the grass, and Kevin followed him.

"That was hysterical," said Randy. "You got the dog to run away in two seconds flat!"

"Why'd you kick him?" asked Talbot.

The waters rose quickly.

"She didn't kick him," said Oak. At least someone had been watching.

"He was coming after my feet." I could feel myself start to hyperventilate.

Kevin returned with the stupid dog in tow. "I'd like everyone to sit down again."

The wet grass seeped through my pants. I hoped that when I got up, it wouldn't look like I had gone to the bathroom.

"Like I said, these dogs have a history," said Kevin. "It's our job to take that experience and figure out the best way to relate to the animal."

"I didn't kick the dog," I said. My caffeine buzz was wearing off, as was my patience with that girl with the pink hair. Who did she think she was, pointing a finger at me without even knowing me?

"Yes, you did," said Talbot.

I was tired of being quiet—tired of being wrongly accused. Everyone thought I was violent anyway. Wasn't that what they were saying about me?

Before I knew it, I'd sprung to my feet, heat emanating from my body. I towered over her. I had all the power. Leaning down toward her, I watched with satisfaction as she cowered.

"I didn't kick the dog," I practically spat in her face. Adrenaline coursed through my body.

Before I knew it, Kevin was occupying what little space remained between the two of us. "That's enough, Iris. Come sit over here."

My heart was still thumping as he led me to my new seat between Oak and Randy.

"She didn't mean to make contact with the dog," Kevin said to Talbot. "What I saw was someone who was perhaps a bit nervous shuffle her feet when an eighty-pound pit bull approached. Now let's end this."

I couldn't have said it better.

"However," said Kevin.

Oh, boy.

"Knowing Roman's history, we have to remember that his owner was abusive. When he would go to lift his leg, it more often than not came down on Roman's back. Or as a kick to the face. So the dog is reacting to his own experience. Our job is to retrain these dogs to trust humans. We need to rewrite their histories so that they see us as the good guys and not as the enemy."

Rewriting history? What a joke. It wasn't even possible. Didn't Kevin know that everyone wanted to rewrite history? Everyone had something in their past that they wished they could make disappear. Of course I would have liked to rewrite history so that I passed my English final and I didn't have to spend the summer here. If I could, I'd go back in time and make it so that Mrs. Schneider never found my list, or, better yet, make it so that my mom never got in that car two years ago.

"What about the rest of them?" asked Randy, Tinkerbelle resting in his lap.

Kevin knew all of their histories. "Well, Bruce here was a street dog. He was found extremely emaciated. We don't know if he ever had a real home. And Persia's owner"—he motioned toward Oak's German shepherd—"was a drug dealer. Persia came to us with a bullet in his shoulder. You'll notice he has a bit of a limp. And Tinkerbelle, well, she was a prize-winning breeding dog forced to litter puppies year after year."

"Is that why she has those funny things dangling from her?" asked Randy.

"Those are teats," I said.

"It's where she produced milk," added Kevin.

Randy looked down to further inspect. "Gross!" He lifted the dog off of his lap.

"Did you grow up on a farm?" asked Oak.

I realized I must have sounded strange to be so scared of dogs and yet know random names for their anatomy. "Animal Planet junkie," I said quietly.

He nodded as though he understood exactly what I meant. "History Channel buff," he whispered back.

I smiled.

Kevin continued, "So what do you say? Are you up for the challenge of getting these dogs trained?"

"Do we have a choice?" asked Randy.

"There's always a choice," said Kevin. He handed me Roman's leash again. This time, when the dog came to smell my feet, I stayed very still, as you're supposed to do with bees. Roman looked like he was inhaling my shoelaces through his nostrils, sniffing intently. But then he decided he was done and had a seat next to me, his head resting on his front paws.

"What are we doing today?" asked Shelley.

"Just getting to know our dogs. Getting to know each other. And we'll learn how to hold a leash. So everyone stand up," said Kevin.

Did he think we were idiots? How hard could it be to hold a leash?

"There is a proper way. I'll use Bruce as an example." Kevin borrowed Shelley's dog. "So this is how it works. Leashes don't work when you hold them like this," he said, demonstrating the way we were all casually holding them. "They only work if you hold them like this."

He took the loop of the leash handle in his right hand and then held the leash with his left. "This is how you tell a dog that you're in control."

"Why doesn't this work?" asked Talbot. Her dog was way out in front of her, and Talbot had her forefinger casually hooked around the leash.

"Because your dog is leading you. He's telling you that he is the boss, but *you* need to be the boss in order for him to feel safe."

"Do you really think this little thing thinks it's the boss of me?" said Randy, regarding the pint-sized Chihuahua at his feet. "I could sit on it and practically end its life!"

"Randy!" screamed Talbot.

"What? Are you going to report me to PETA? I'm just telling it like it is," said Randy.

"Your dog doesn't respect you yet, Randy," said Kevin.

"How do you know?" asked Randy.

Kevin pointed toward the dog. "See how she's sitting with her back toward you, totally not in tune with what you might want her to be doing?"

"I thought she was just sunbathing," said Randy.

"Watch this." Kevin gave Bruce's leash to Oak, who looked a little lost with a dog on each arm, and went over to Tinkerbelle. Kevin took the leash, holding it with his right hand looped and his left hand holding the leash and gave a slight tug. Tinkerbelle abruptly stood up and came around to face Kevin.

"That is being in control of your dog. That's how you properly hold a leash. Now I want you all to try." Kevin handed Tinkerbelle's leash back to Randy.

I tried to hold the leash as Kevin had shown us, but Roman didn't budge.

"Face me!" I said to my dog, whose ears perked up right away as though he fully understood my command—but instead of calmly turning his attention toward me as Kevin had demonstrated, Roman began yanking on the leash. I held on tightly to the other end, paying particular attention to how close my feet were coming to him because the last thing I wanted to do was make him think that I was about to beat him up like his previous owner.

"Give just a little tug." Kevin looked on, and I listened and jerked ever so slightly on the leash. Like magic, Roman perked up and turned around to look at me. Everyone else was still struggling with this exercise.

"Great work, Iris!" said Kevin.

I felt like I had the magic touch. Garrett was rolling on his back, and Persia was having a light snack of fresh grass. Their dogs were being ornery.

Nothing had gone my way like this in a long time. Not my bike wheels staying inflated. Not summer school being avoided. Not mothers staying alive. Nothing. But just now, I'd experienced what it felt like for things to go well.

"Your dog had an accident," announced Talbot.

I looked down. There on the grass was one of the largest dog dumps in all of dog-dump history.

"You need a bag?" Kevin asked, pulling a blue plastic baggie from his back pocket.

"For what?" I played dumb.

"The poop." This got everyone else's attention, and they stopped what they were doing to watch the showdown.

"What poop?" I asked.

"Iris, I'm not stupid. Here's the bag." His tone seemed to have shifted from supportive to admonishing. I was embarrassed. I wished everyone would just focus on their own dogs and stop staring at me.

"I'm not cleaning up poop," I said quietly. I wasn't about to let myself be degraded in such a demeaning way, forced to pick up poop from this animal that I didn't even like, while everyone watched like I was some sort of circus act.

"It's part of the deal," said Kevin. "If you're not sure how to do it, I can show you."

"Who doesn't know how to pick up a dump?" asked Randy.

Everyone laughed, and *I felt the waters rise swiftly all the way to my neck.* Why was the world out to embarrass me? I contemplated just walking away from it all. But before my body had time to react, Roman took off again. In my anger, I'd let go of his leash. I chased after him, shouting his name. And, to my surprise, he stopped running and waited for me.

"Thank you," I mouthed to him as I picked up the leash and walked back to the group, grabbing the small doggie bag out of Kevin's hand. I approached the offending area. Sticking my hand in the bag, I picked up the poop, still warm through the plastic. I twisted the bag and waved it around, showing everyone I *was* capable of picking up dog poop. As I tossed the bag in the trash, Talbot came up to me with her dog. I wondered what the next rude thing to come out of her mouth was going to be.

"Sorry about all that," said Talbot.

"Sorry about what?" I wasn't about to let her have the satisfaction of knowing she had angered and embarrassed me…twice.

"It's this thing I do. When I'm uncomfortable, I find someone to pick on. That someone was you." She paused. "I'm working on it."

Her candor impressed me. When I made a mistake, I blew it off or pretended it never happened, but Talbot was willing to face her gaffes head on. It made it easy to forgive her.

"Do you like your dog? I could just take mine home with me!" She let Garrett lick her face.

"I'm not so into dogs," I said.

"Well, what are you into?" she asked.

I shrugged. I didn't even know anymore. I guess lately I was into composing hit lists and making court appearances.

"That guy seems like a jerk." I motioned toward Randy, who was looking my way and laughing at me—probably for the whole dog poop situation.

"Don't let him piss you off. He's nothing but a bully. I can tell. And she"—Talbot pointed to Shelley, who was sitting on the grass with Bruce, pulling up grass at the roots and then chewing on them—"she's on her own planet. At least that guy seems nice. And maybe even cute if he ever took off that thing."

I looked over at Oak. I wasn't the only one wondering what he'd look like without the hood.

"He never takes it off," I said.

"You know him?"

"We go to Santa Cruz High. But I've never even talked to him before today."

"Hey, what are you doing after this? It is summer vacation, right? There's gotta be some fun to be had," said Talbot.

"I have to head home," I said.

"Parents?"

"Yeah." I didn't get into the fact that at my place it was just *parent*, nor did I tell her that my afternoon would consist of preparing dinner for myself, and then a whole lot of nature TV. Dad would no doubt be working late. I was happy to learn that his date with Janet had been a bust.

Talbot shrugged. "Well, maybe another time. My dad's always riding me about bringing home a 'decent and respectable' friend."

"Um, don't forget you met me at juvenile community service," I said.

"Hey, it's better than some of the other people I've been hanging out with, believe you me."

Kevin interrupted us. "Okay, gang. You've taken in a lot today:

met your dogs, learned about leash leading. And," he said, glancing over at me, "some of you were even educated on the various methods of picking up canine excrement. All in all, a full afternoon. If you could bring your dogs to the van and then take their leashes off, I'll see you all again tomorrow."

I had made it through day one. Only twenty-nine more to go.

Not that I was counting.

six

Doug Loggins, my court-appointed therapist, didn't get much out of me that first day. He kept waiting for me to speak, as if I had anything to say. Somehow, we ended up chatting about my favorite juice combinations that Dad had brought home, as though the medley of beet-carrot-apple juice contained some deep commentary about my psyche.

"Well, this was good," Doug said when our time was up. "But next time, let's focus less on vegetables and more on your anger."

I left embarrassed and dreaded my next office visit.

That first week of dog training inched forward. Because summer school didn't start until Thursday, I was able to sleep in a few days more (once Dad was done puttering around the house early in the morning).

I wore my running shoes every day to work with the dogs so I'd be armed and ready to bolt as fast as my legs would take me if things got scary. Within the first couple of days, I had successfully taught Roman how to walk and stay on a leash, always exercising caution. He had a habit of bringing his nose to my hand when I praised him, which made me uncomfortable, so as soon as he'd perform a task successfully, I'd lift my hand to mess with my hair, scratch my face—anything to have it unavailable for Roman's wet-nose press. He'd look at me with his sad eyes.

"Let's stick to the lesson," I'd tell him.

By Wednesday, it seemed as though everyone had become best friends with their dogs, except for me. Even Randy and Tinkerbelle were hitting it off, playing tug of war with a stick. It was a hot day, and Kevin brought out some spray bottles. The dogs were having fun getting wet. When I sprayed water in Roman's face, he tried to bite it. Go figure.

"Hang out after this?" asked Talbot from across the grass, rolling around on the ground with her dog.

"I can't. I have plans," I lied.

I couldn't manage the friends I had (if they still considered themselves my friends), let alone forge ahead with a new friendship. Yesterday afternoon I'd caught a glimpse of Ashley when I rode by Pergolesi after dog training. She was bringing someone an iced coffee drink on the wraparound porch. I'm pretty sure she saw me because she started to lift her hand up to wave, but then, as though her instincts got the best of her, her hand froze at waist level, and I turned the corner.

"Suit yourself," Talbot said, turning her attention back to her dog. "You'd hang out with me this weekend, wouldn't you, Garrett?" She was lying on her back as her dog stood over her, and she rubbed his belly. The dog loved it and started kicking its hind leg repeatedly in pleasure.

I walked Roman to a shady spot and tried my best to imitate Talbot's body position and laidback attitude. From my vantage point on my back, Roman looked even bigger and more intimidating, but if this is how one played with a dog, I was going to give it a try. He responded to my new positioning right away, coming over to check it out. He nudged me with his nose. It tickled. I gently pushed him back. He didn't get the message and came at me again, this time jabbing me in the hip.

"No!" I said.

But my commands weren't working.

Roman let out a subtle growl, and before I could stand up, he grabbed my shorts and began tugging, his growl turning into a full-on snarl.

"Help!" I screamed. I covered my face with my arms, hoping to save my face if he launched into an assault.

Within seconds, Kevin was at my side, in control of the leash and the dog at the other end of it. When all was clear, I stood up, shaken.

"What were you doing?" he asked me. Roman had seemed to snap back to his listening self.

"I was trying to play with him, like Talbot's doing with her dog."

"She has a very different dog," said Kevin.

"I see that."

"They don't play the same way," Kevin said.

I couldn't keep it all straight. I'd finally made an effort to work with my dog, and he'd tried to eat me.

Kevin had Roman lie down while he explained more dog rules to me. "By lying down on the ground, on your back, you are completely submitting to Roman. You're letting him know that he's the boss of you and that he's in charge of the game."

"That was his version of a game?" I asked.

"Did you think he was attacking you?" asked Kevin.

I burst into tears. Oak came over and took Roman's leash from Kevin, who put his arms around me while I blubbered into his chest.

"It's okay. He won't hurt you," he whispered into my ear. "You have to learn to trust him. And in the meantime, no lying down on your back, okay?"

I nodded.

"You sure?" asked Kevin.

"As long as you're positive he wasn't trying to eat me," I said.

"I promise. We feed them a good breakfast before they work with you."

Talbot and her dog were still both lounging together, and she turned my way and smirked as if to say: *This whole thing could have been avoided if you'd just committed to making plans with me.*

I was determined not to be late on the first day of summer school. I had been so efficient, in fact, that I rolled Dad's bike into its parking spot thirty minutes early. Good timing had never been my forte. There was only so much roaming of the halls I could do before I got bored and headed toward my classroom, and besides, the more people I came across, the greater the chance they would recognize me as that girl who went nuts. Scanning my enrollment papers, I found my classroom assignment: C-123. Schneider's room, which was more like a tomb.

Just great.

She'd never be my teacher again, but the thought of even setting foot in that classroom made me sick.

Even though most remnants of her presence had been removed, above the whiteboard, still tacked to the wall, was the quote by Molière. Who was this Molière, and why was he giving such import to grammar anyway? Probably some historical English teacher famous for torturing his students.

Inside the classroom was just one other student, searching for something in a green canvas army bag. I took a seat at the back of the room, ready to become a wallflower as soon as class began.

"Why don't you take a seat at the front. It's going to be a small group, I think," said this apparently know-it-all, bossy student.

Who in the world did this girl think she was, telling me where to sit? I felt anger-fueled adrenaline race through my body, but I worked hard to suppress it, knowing that acting out in any way would not be the best way to mark my big return to school.

"I'm good here, thanks," I said.

"I'm Perry," said the girl. "I'll be your teacher for this class."

What? How did a kid get this job? She must have been some honor student or something—looking to perk up her college application form. Was that even legal? But as she came closer to shake my hand, I saw she wasn't my age at all.

"I look young," she said almost apologetically.

"I thought you were in the class," I said.

"Well, I am—it's just that I also happen to be teaching it."

A teacher who introduced herself by her first name? I was impressed.

"Iris," I said.

She paused and looked up, like she was recalling some information. "Iris Moody, right?" Why did she know my last name? What had she heard about me? I was probably blacklisted throughout the school. *Watch out for this one. Don't piss her off; she'll add you to her list.*

I was so embarrassed.

"I've studied my roster," she said and handed me a syllabus entitled: "Fairy Tales: Happily Ever After?"

"Am I in the right class? English 3?"

Perry nodded her head. "Yes."

I'd read all the fairy tales I ever wanted to read in the second grade. Mom bought me a huge collection, and I remembered staring at that glossy cover when she read from it. All of the characters from the stories were there, Rapunzel sitting on Cinderella's coach, a leprechaun in her lap. Puss in Boots standing next to Rumpelstiltskin and Bluebeard's facial hair weaving its way across the page like a piece of yarn gone wild. We'd cuddle on the couch, and Mom would make me a cup of chamomile tea and place a handmade quilt on top of me. If the stories ever got too scary, I'd hide beneath, as though shielding my eyes would turn off my imagination. They were all good memories, those fairy tales, but they were stories for young kids, not for high schoolers.

"Do you think you could help me move some chairs around?" Perry asked. "We're going to get rid of these pesky rows and make a circle."

I felt obligated more than ever to be the best student I could be, as though that might erase my current reputation. This could be my chance to start over.

✿

In a short while, students filed into the classroom, taking their seats at various vacancies in the circle that Perry and I had assembled. The seats on either side of me remained empty.

When Lorrie Hastings, swim team snob, ambled in late, Perry motioned for her to go to one of the free seats next to me.

"I am not sitting next to *her*." Lorrie snickered.

The waters percolated inside. How dare she embarrass me in front of the whole class? It would be so easy to reach out and teach her a lesson. It was almost what was expected of me now.

"Lorrie, is it?" asked Perry.

Lorrie nodded.

"You make one more comment like that in here, and you are out. This classroom will be a place of respect."

Perry was protecting me. I hadn't felt as though anyone had been on my side in a long, long time.

Lorrie rolled her eyes and reluctantly sat down next to me.

The circle setup was awful because I couldn't hide behind anyone. We were all equally visible. As I looked around the classroom, I recognized a few familiar faces—one guy from PE, another from biology, a few from Mrs. Schneider's English class. They were all students who failed. And now I was one of them.

Perry addressed the class. "So you might be wondering why I have chosen fairy tales as the focus for our class this summer."

"Fairy tales!" the boy next to me said. "That's girlie stuff."

"If by 'girlie' you mean mass murder, infanticide, and lust, then yes, by all means, very girlie," said Perry.

The guy next to me looked perplexed—in fact, we all did, not quite sure what she was talking about. But any teacher who uttered the word *lust* was bound to get our attention.

"Since you are getting a year's worth of credit for a six-week course, I'm not going to lie—it's very intense. Not only will you have to complete all of the required material in your reader, but you will each need to read and review an outside collection of fairy tales as well as compose an eight- to ten-page research paper on your chosen collection in relation to a specific topic."

I stopped listening at the phrase *eight- to ten-page research paper*, focusing only on the five-hundred-page reader plopped on the desk in front of me and the syllabus, thick with explanations. High school seemed to be all about following directions. I had grown tired of listening.

Perry spoke as though she had been reading my mind. "Keep in mind that this syllabus is a formality. The school requires that I churn one out. But in this class, in addition to hard work and a firmer grasp of the English language, we're going to have fun. We're going to delve into deep psychological recesses and explore these tropes that come up again and again in this type of literature."

"What's a trope?" asked a girl dressed in gothic garb across from me.

It seemed as though Perry had forgotten that we were all here because we had failed English class. Instead, she talked to us like we were honor students.

Perry said, "The valiant prince, the girl who gets punished for being curious, the missing mother."

My ears perked up with that last phrase.

"These are all tropes that we will be discussing in detail—that is to say, these leitmotifs occur again and again in these stories, and we're here to act as psychologists, sociologists, and historians to figure out why." Perry looked suddenly lost in thought. She stared above the whiteboard.

We looked around at one another, wondering if our teacher would ever return to us.

"What's wrong?" asked the guy from my PE class.

Perry kept her eyes fixed on Schneider's Molière quote.

"Something is going to have to be done about that," she said. She dragged a chair over to the back wall, hoisted herself up, ripped the butcher paper with the quote from the wall, crumpled it into a ball, and slam-dunked it into the recycling bin. Score two points for Perry, zero for Mrs. Schneider.

I had been staring at that quote for two years wishing I could have done that very same thing.

English, even if it was only temporary, had just become my favorite subject.

❁

At our session Thursday after school, Doug Loggins asked me what my "exit plan" was when I got angry.

"What do you mean?"

"Well, if you don't have one in place, we need to develop a strategy, something that interrupts the anger—that makes you walk away from situations if using your words isn't an option."

I had seen evacuation plans posted in plenty of hotel rooms, but never did I think I would need my own.

"I have to go to the bathroom," I said, uncomfortable with this session topic.

"Go right ahead," said Doug, "if that's how you want to spend this time."

I was nearly at the door when it occurred to me that I had used the bathroom as an excuse to escape the session.

I turned back around and faced Doug. "I don't really have to go. That was just me showcasing my exit strategy."

"See, Iris, you're coming a long way here," said Doug.

I sat back down and finished the session.

At home, I felt exhausted, and there was little more I could do than collapse on the couch and watch my animal shows until Dad came home. When he arrived, he was carrying a work suit encased in plastic wrapping.

"What's that?" I asked.

"My promotion suit. If they're gonna give me the position, I've gotta look the part, right?"

"I guess," I said. My show was just getting to an interesting part about a battle between two disputing ant colonies living in the rain forest in South America. The dominant colony had taken in prisoners to work as slaves. For a moment there, I had forgotten it was even a show about ants at all—it looked just like some epic Hollywood blockbuster. But Dad was making so much noise taking the plastic off the suit that I got up to take a closer look.

"It's an Armani," he said proudly.

Dad had never been one to care about brand names before.

"What does that mean?" I asked.

"It means it's expensive."

I looked at the price tag dangling from the sleeve. Fifteen hundred dollars.

"Sheesh! No kidding!" Here I was using his bike because he refused to get me a working secondhand replacement while he was splurging on clothes.

"You leave the finances to me, Iris. My new salary can afford me this suit, and if you get through the summer without getting into trouble, I will get you a brand-new bike. Any kind you want."

He had said the magic words. I had been dreaming about a black Pake Urban six-speed for years. I would keep my mouth shut about his suit.

The phone rang, cutting our conversation short.

"It's for you," said my dad.

"Who is it?"

"She says her name is Talbot. Who's Talbot?"

"Dog training friend," I said, grabbing the phone. "What's up?" I made my way to the private confines of my bedroom.

"I got your number from Kevin. I was wondering if you wanted to come over for dinner tomorrow?"

Though I had refused her past invitations, I was glad she had called. Maybe it would be refreshing to have a new friend who didn't know about the recent events of my past. Someone who thought I still had a mother.

I asked Dad if I could go.

"You just met her," was his response.

"But we'll be spending the next five weeks together."

Dad put the plastic covering back on his suit. "Well, what did she do to land herself there?"

"I don't know," I said. "But if it was really bad, she'd be in jail."

He nodded, carefully hanging his new suit in his closet.

I ran back to my room.

"I'm in!" I said.

"Yeah!" said Talbot. It felt good to have a friend actually cheer at the prospect of hanging out with me.

seven

At the park on Friday, it was Kevin who was running late. The rest of us sat in the grass waiting for him to arrive. A cool breeze passed through, and the fog hadn't quite lifted that afternoon.

"Knock-knock. Anyone home?" said Talbot, rapping on Oak's covered head.

He pulled the strings tighter so that his hood practically enveloped his entire face.

Randy plopped down next to me. "Where do you go to school?"

"Santa Cruz High," I said. "So does Hood—" I stopped myself from saying *Hoodie Boy* and corrected myself. "So does Oak."

"Me, too," said Randy. "Just graduated."

I couldn't believe I had gone to the same school but had never even noticed him.

"I'm starting my junior year at Santa Cruz High," said Shelley.

"How is it we've never seen each other before?" I asked.

"Maybe we have?" said Shelley.

In my head I ran through all of my classes from the previous year and inserted a visual image of Shelley. But her presence in my classes wasn't ringing a bell.

"How about you, Talbot? You a Cardinal, too?" asked Randy.

"First of all, that has to be close to the lamest mascot ever, and no, I don't go to SC, I go to Clark Academy."

Randy and Oak both reacted by rolling their eyes.

"Whoa, fancy pants. Well, excuse me," said Randy.

"It's not like that," she said. "I'm not like that."

Clark Academy was where the rich kids went. They lived in big houses and wore uniforms and their parents bought them brand-new cars as soon as they turned sixteen. You could tell a kid went to Clark just by the car they rolled down Pacific Avenue on a Friday night.

"What kind of car you drive?" asked Randy. I could tell he was eager to get under her skin.

"I used to drive a beat-up BMW," Talbot said.

"Figures," said Randy.

"But I don't drive it anymore."

"Daddy took it away?" teased Randy.

Talbot looked him straight in the eyes. "More like, daughter totaled it drunk driving."

My stomach clenched, thinking about how my mom had been killed by a drunk driver in Topanga Canyon. I didn't know much about the guy who killed her. Dad didn't want me at his sentencing. All I knew was that he was sitting in jail—maybe for life.

And here I was, not far behind his path: my own court hearing under my belt, paying my dues for my own crime. I wondered if anyone had been hurt in Talbot's drunken accident. What innocent victim had she affected? Whose life had she forever changed?

"Was anyone hurt?" I had to ask.

"Just yours truly. Concussed head. Shattered glass. Broken arm." She pointed to her arm, which was covered in a smattering of scars, reminding me of Roman's battered fur.

"You could have killed someone," said Oak.

"Okay, Mother Teresa, what brought you here?" Talbot asked Oak.

"Stealing," he said.

"That's original," she said. "What did you take? Sweatshirts?" She tried to pry his hood off, but he moved out of the way just before she could reach him.

"I hacked into people's credit card accounts and stole enough money to help out this nonprofit my buddy was working for."

Incognito computer genius meets Robin Hood. I was intrigued.

"No way!" said Randy. "That's awesome! You're a computer nerd!"

"It wasn't so awesome once the Feds caught on."

"The Feds?" asked Shelley.

"Yeah, I guess they thought I was the leader of a big hacking ring they'd been trying to nab for years. They felt pretty stupid that it was just me—a sixteen-year-old working out of my bedroom."

The lines were so blurred between good and bad. I mean, Oak's objective had been really benevolent. And in my own situation, there had been no malicious intent—yet here we were, branded as trouble.

"What did you do?" Talbot asked Shelley, taking a marker to her already decorated high-tops and adding squiggles and hearts.

"Graffiti. On a few highway overpasses. Cops caught us."

"Do you know someone named Scott?" I asked, remembering the guy who was sentenced before me at the courthouse.

Shelley's eyes widened. "Scott Haydon? Hell, yeah! He's like the king of the wet wall! You know Scott?"

"I saw his trial. It was right before mine. The judge did not like him."

Shelley laughed. "Nobody likes him. Not even his friends. They're all scared of him."

"What about you, Randy? Punch anyone?" asked Talbot.

Randy got a solemn look on his face. "Worse."

"What did you do?" asked Shelley.

"C'mon, tell us," said Talbot.

He leaned in close, and we all mirrored his body language. "I killed someone," he whispered.

Before I could control my breath, I gasped and looked at Talbot.

"That's some heavy stuff, man. Does Kevin know you did that?" Oak seemed genuinely concerned. "Are you sure you're even supposed to be out of jail?"

Randy started laughing out of control. "You guys! I'm just joking!" His laughter grew. "I didn't kill no one! But you all believed me!"

Talbot was the first to laugh. Then Oak. Shelley and I were both hesitant.

"So what did you really do?" I asked.

"I pulled a knife on a guy in a fight. But I never used it on him. I should have, though, because apparently you still get time just for 'brandishing a weapon.' This whole system is so stupid. I've already had two misdemeanors. And now that I'm eighteen, it's serious jail time if I do anything else. I mean, do I look like an angel?"

"Do any of us?" asked Shelley. When she spoke, she didn't look at us but at some far-off place. Here was a person who seemed to be more in her own head than I was.

Talbot gazed down at her mismatched shoes—one black and one green. We were a group of mismatched misfits, all here for very different reasons, now forced to work toward a common goal.

"What are you in for?" Randy asked me. I should have known this was coming, but it still managed to take me by surprise. Up until now I hadn't had to explain to anyone what I'd done. I hated the way it felt, this invasion of privacy.

My heart raced. I could feel *the waters start to swell* and my cheeks flush. I wanted to run and hide, but I knew I couldn't. I had to answer Randy's question. Everyone else had fessed up. Why was this so hard for me?

"I wrote a hit list." I watched their eyes widen. "It was just in my journal. Just for my eyes—a list of people I hated at that moment. I might have said I wanted to kill a teacher. People at school thought I was really planning on going through with it."

As scared as I was to confess the truth to the group, they had all been brave enough to share with me. They weren't going to be judgmental or act superior, since they had experienced something similar.

I continued, "Then there was this teacher—she found the list, and I tried to get the book back, and I accidentally hurt her."

Randy jumped to his feet. "You're the one who attacked Mrs. Schneider? You're like a legend! I can't believe that was you! People have been wanting to kick her ass for years!" Randy looked starstruck.

"It was totally unfair." Oak jumped in.

I remembered seeing him that morning, sitting next to me.

Oak continued, "Mrs. Schneider had it out for you that day. She knew you weren't cheating—she just wanted to bust someone for something. Since when is it a crime to express how you feel? That whole thing was total censorship, if you ask me."

I was so thrilled that someone else understood what had really happened that day.

Just then Kevin appeared out of the rec center building, walking our five dogs on their leashes. Between Roman's missing leg and Tinkerbelle's pathetic pint-sized body and the drool oozing out of Bruce's mouth, they looked like a particularly sorry bunch.

I wondered if the dogs were thinking the same thing about us—that we were all a bunch of strays.

"Sorry I'm late, guys," Kevin said while doling out a dog to each of us. The only one ecstatic to see her dog was Talbot, of course. I hesitantly took Roman's leash and tried to stay calm when he came over to sniff me. He found a spot on the grass and leaned into my body, the nub of his missing leg resting on my bare calf. It was so gross, but I was too afraid to shift my position, worried that he may see it as a sign of aggression and defensively attack.

"So what do these animals all have in common?" asked Kevin.

"They're dogs," answered Randy.

Obviously.

"Aside from that," said Kevin.

"They're super cute!" said Talbot, scratching Garrett between the ears. How was it that she was so at ease around dogs?

"They're mean," offered Shelley.

"*Mean* implies that they know what nice is and that they are choosing not to be nice," Kevin said. "What I'd suggest to all of you is that dogs who have been through the sorts of traumas these dogs have are always in survival mode. Eat or be eaten."

"Kill or be killed," I added. I couldn't help myself. Pit bulls were ferocious. Even ones with missing appendages. I didn't care what Kevin said.

Kevin was hell-bent on driving home his point. "You have to remember that these dogs weren't born this way. They learned this behavior—and if they can learn it, then they can unlearn it. So that's our job."

"So they're going to school to 'unlearn,'" said Randy.

"Precisely. These dogs are now all spayed and neutered, which helps," said Kevin.

I knew that this could drastically reduce aggression, especially in males.

"I know a few guys who could use some neutering," said Talbot. I wondered who she was talking about. I knew of one ex-boyfriend named Andy Dunn I'd like to add to that list!

Kevin talked over our laughter. "So there are a few different types of aggression, but the ones we're going to focus on are dominance and fear."

"Wait, so you're trying to tell me that puny little Tinkerbelle here has an aggression issue?" asked Randy.

"Absolutely."

Randy shook his head. "Hers has to be fear. She's got to be afraid of everything! I mean, she kind of should be, considering her size and all."

"Actually, hers is dominance-based," said Kevin. "She is particularly food aggressive. If you go anywhere near her when she's eating, or if another dog gets in her space, she'll attack."

"Thatta girl," said Randy. Tinkerbelle rolled over on her back.

"Most of the dogs here have dominance-based aggression. Except for Roman," said Kevin.

Of course. My dog would be the exception.

"His issues are fear-based."

Roman was apparently afraid of everything, and the person who was supposed to get him over his fears was afraid of him. We were a perfect couple.

"And Iris, if your dog still doesn't listen, you need to do an adjustment," said Kevin.

"How do I do that?" I asked.

"Keep control of the leash and bring your thumb and middle finger to the dog's rear and gently place some pressure on it."

I watched Kevin do this, and Roman immediately sat down.

"Don't forget to praise your dog!" Kevin reminded us.

When it was our turn, we each found our own area of grass to work on.

"I think my dog has rabies!" I heard Shelley say. Her bulldog was constantly gathering large amounts of foamy saliva at the sides of his mouth and compulsively drooling.

"That's just the breed!" shouted Kevin. "He comes from a long line of droolers."

Roman was doing pretty well on the leash. He wasn't pulling or tugging as badly as the day before. I decided to try my hand at making him sit.

"Sit." I said. It came out as a whisper. I tried again. "Sit!"

Roman stopped walking and looked at me. But all three legs stayed standing on the grass. I attempted a correction, bringing my fingers over Roman's back. But before they could make contact with his fur, he began growling and snarling and jumped (on his one hind leg) up to my arm, which, in my state of panic, I was able to move out of the way quickly enough. I dropped the leash and ran toward Kevin, who was already moving quickly in my direction.

"I'm done dealing with that dog!" I yelled at him. I didn't know if I wanted to cry or kick something. I felt humiliated. Defeated. Scared. How many more times was this dog going to intimidate me?

I walked over to a big cypress tree and sat down, leaning on the flaky bark. I watched as Kevin tugged and yanked on the leash until whatever anger had possessed Roman passed and he snapped back to reality. Kevin walked him to the office and then came back out to me.

"What did you do with him?" I asked.

"I think he's had enough for the day. It's not an easy process for him."

For him! What about for me? How could the dog be both an aggressor and a victim? It didn't make sense!

I looked at Kevin. "Considering the fact that he almost bit my arm off, shouldn't you be mad at him instead of feel sorry for him?"

"But I do feel sorry for him. He's been through a lot. Remember, he was abused. Beaten repeatedly. When you brought your hand down, did you bring it over his head where he could see it? Or over his back?"

I tried to remember. "Over his back, I guess."

"That was probably it," said Kevin.

"So it was my fault?"

"I'm not placing blame," said Kevin. "I just want you to start viewing things the way Roman sees them. When he saw a hand coming out of nowhere, from his own life experience, it was a signal that he was about to get beaten up. The hand wasn't a part of you. Do you understand?"

Nothing made sense anymore. Trying to understand this dog was a waste of time. "I guess."

"So you know what you have to do next time?"

Next time! Did he seriously believe there was going to be a next time?

"Can't I have a new dog?" I asked.

"Roman needs you," said Kevin.

"Can't I switch with someone else?"

"Roman needs *you*."

"Why do you keep saying that?" I asked.

"It's no coincidence you two are paired up together. I think you have a lot more in common than you realize," said Kevin. Then he left to help the rest of the group with their dogs.

The waters were rising, churning in my stomach like rough ocean waves. Why were this dog's needs more important than my own?

❁

"That was heavy," said Talbot, once the other dogs had been collected and we were officially dismissed.

"I'm over it," I announced.

"Over what?" Talbot asked.

"That dog."

"He's so cute!" said Talbot.

"You think everyone is cute," I said.

"You should see me with guys."

We laughed.

"So, you coming to my place tonight?" asked Talbot.

"Yup. Can I bike there?"

"You better take the bus. It's up a steep hill at the top of Bay."

"What time?"

"Seven. And don't be late. My parents are nuts about dinner starting on time. Speaking of which, there's my dad. See ya!" She ran off and hopped into her dad's car.

Tonight, I would be having a real family dinner.

As I was unlocking my bike, Oak approached me. "I think I would have been scared, too," he said.

"Of what?" I pretended not to know what he was talking about.

"Actually, all things considered, you stayed pretty calm. A lot calmer than I would have been."

"I don't really like dogs," I said.

He loosened the hood around his face, exposing his chin. "The queen of the animal kingdom doesn't like dogs? How's that for ironic?"

I never would have expected the word *ironic* to come out of Oak's mouth. He was the school bad boy—not that I thought he'd be speaking in grunts or anything.

"You wanna go to Pergolesi and grab a coffee?" he asked, straight out of left field.

He knew about my passion for bio and my love affair with coffee? This guy was observant.

"I do, but I can't," I said. "I have homework. Summer school. And then I have dinner plans. Rain check?"

"Sure."

I nodded and Oak waved and got into his truck—an old, faded, cherry-red Chevrolet.

On my bike ride home I wondered if Oak was just being nice to me because a three-legged professional killer almost attacked me—or if maybe, just maybe, he kinda liked me? I couldn't decode Kevin's message about Roman and me—how we apparently had a lot in common. Besides both being mammals, I couldn't think of one thing. Roman had fear-based aggression. What was I afraid of? I guess I didn't love speaking my mind, but I still got frustrated when people didn't get where I was coming from.

In a way, Roman had it a lot harder than me—he didn't have the capacity to communicate. I, at least, had the ability to open up to people, should I ever choose to do so.

At home the neighbor's dog was at the fence, greeting me with growls and barks. I gathered the mail from our box, tucked the pile of bills under my arm, and approached the dog with a display of fake confidence.

I looked around to see if anyone was watching me. The dog followed me closely, never breaking eye contact.

In a stern voice I said, "Sit!" I watched his ears perk up as the ninety-pound bullmastiff lowered his body into a quintessential dog sitting position.

I couldn't help but smile.

"Stay!" I said, putting my hand up to his face on the other side of the fence.

The dog didn't move until I was through my front door.

At least one animal was listening to me.

❋

After completing two hours of reading for Perry's class (it took me that long because I kept getting distracted, thinking about Oak), bouncing around on the Internet, and Googling Oak's name (his court case came up in a small article in the *Sentinel* with the headline, "Local Teen Genius Leads Police on a Cyber Goose Chase"), it was finally time to head over to Talbot's. I checked the fridge to see if I could bring anything to contribute to dinner. It was pretty barren except for a few vegetable juices and a bottle of champagne that Dad had purchased—no doubt to celebrate his impending promotion. The final interview was on Monday, and I couldn't wait until he stopped talking about it all the time.

Even though Talbot had told me not to bike, I tried to cycle up Bay, one of the biggest hills in the city, until my legs felt like they were on fire, at which point I waited patiently for the 1 University bus to arrive and hooked my bike to the front. The bus dropped me off right in front of Talbot's house at UC Santa Cruz's faculty housing. I guessed her parents were professors.

The brown houses with green trim all looked the same, like a mini suburbia. Across the housing development were two huge fields of dried grass, cut in half by the road that the bus continued on up to campus. Cows grazed on the grass, and at the top of the hill were scores of redwood trees clustered in tight circles. Hidden among the shade of the redwoods sat UC Santa Cruz. It felt strange to be in such proximity to a university and yet, with my slipping grades and out-of-school problems, I couldn't have felt further away from a college-bound future. I would feel like a complete failure if I didn't make it to my vision of the Brown library.

I walked my bike up to Talbot's and rang the doorbell.

A little boy answered. "I'm Thaddeus, but you can call me Bug Man." He held up a plastic container with all sorts of creepy crawlies in it.

"Thad! Get those bugs out of the house!" Talbot's mom's voice bellowed from the kitchen.

"Cool insects," I said. It made him stop in his tracks.

"You like bugs?" he asked.

"I do!" I said, bending down to get a better look at the smattering of earwigs and potato bugs crawling around in the plastic container. "Did you know that there are over twenty million bugs per person on the planet?"

"No way!" said Talbot's brother.

"It's true," I said.

"That's disgusting." Talbot bounded down the stairs to greet me. "You can put your bike here." She leaned it up against the hallway wall.

"Ah! An environmentalist. I like it," said the man following behind her.

"That's my dad," Talbot said.

I shook his hand. He squeezed it so hard it hurt.

"It's not by choice, Dad. She doesn't have a car."

I stood there and smiled awkwardly.

"Well, that makes two of you then," her dad said and walked into the kitchen.

Did he think that, like his daughter, I had been convicted of drunk driving as well?

Talbot stared at my feet. "We're a no-shoe household. You can put yours in the basket. Mom likes to remind us that she doesn't want everything we've potentially stepped in to follow us home."

"Remind her about the shoes!" shouted her mom from the kitchen.

"On it!" Talbot yelled back.

"Watch your tone!" called her father.

Talbot rolled her eyes.

"You watch your tone…" she said, under her breath. "Come on, I have to set the table."

In the kitchen, I met Talbot's mother, who looked exactly like Talbot but older and without a nose ring. In fact, her parents seemed so completely normal. I didn't know what I was expecting, maybe more piercings and tattoos between the two of them.

I followed Talbot around the table, placing forks and knives on either side of the fabric placemats she was setting down. At our house, we were self-sufficient. Every man for himself.

Dinner was a green-bean-and-tomato salad with mozzarella cheese that melted in my mouth and a huge bowl of pasta with fresh pesto Talbot's dad made from basil growing in their garden. Way better than my usual mac-and-cheese.

"So, Iris, where do you go to school?" asked Talbot's dad.

"Santa Cruz High."

"Do you like it?" asked her mom.

I nodded, lying.

Talbot's dad followed up with, "What does your dad do?"

I hadn't come prepared for an interview.

"He's a manager at a juicing facility," I said.

"And your mom?" asked Talbot's mom.

There was a certain look people gave me when I told them my mom was dead. I could see the pity in their eyes. They'd stare at me an uncomfortably long time and conjure up a specific smile that said both *That is so awful* and *I'm so glad I'm not you.* I wasn't interested in inviting these pity-party smiles to ruin my perfectly good dinner at Talbot's.

"She's a librarian," I said. It was just easier to speak about my mom in the present tense.

"Oh really! Where?" asked Talbot's dad. "Thaddeus, stop playing with your food!"

Talbot's brother disassembled the vegetable village on his plate.

I struggled to remember the name of the library in the center of town that I had walked by so many times. Then it came to me. "Central Branch. On Church." Little did they know that since my mom died, I avoided libraries like the plague.

"So you must be an avid reader then," said Talbot's mother. I didn't mention I had failed English.

"Yeah, and an avid batterer of English teachers," said Talbot, under her breath.

"What was that?" asked her dad.

"Nothing," Talbot said.

I shot her a look.

Talbot's dad wiped pesto off of his lips. "See that, Talbot, some people your age actually enjoy reading literature."

Talbot rolled her eyes and said to me, "He thinks I should do better in school."

"Better is an understatement," added her mother.

I was sitting there privy to a conversation that was meant just for the three of them. It didn't quite feel right, and I could tell it was making Talbot uncomfortable.

Hoping to change the subject, I turned my attention to Thaddeus. "Did you know that in Thailand they eat grasshoppers?" I said.

"Cool! I want to go there!" said Thaddeus.

But Talbot's mom brought the focus back to me. "So what are your college plans?"

"Hopefully, I'll be at Brown. It's where my mom went," I said.

"You set your sights high. I like that," said Talbot's dad. "I wish someone else would do the same." He looked over at Talbot, who refused to make eye contact with him.

Even though it was easy to say I was going to Brown, I knew that in reality, it all depended on my grades and whether or not I'd get a student loan approved at the bank.

"Any idea what you'll study?" asked Talbot's dad.

It was beginning to feel as though I were back on trial with all these questions. Did they always hound Talbot like this? I suddenly appreciated my dad's silence.

Talbot forked her food. "Dad's a psychology professor. He's way into the *thought process*."

"Or in some cases, the lack thereof," her dad said and shot his daughter another look.

They were coming down hard on Talbot, and I could tell by the way she threw down her bread that she'd had enough.

I answered his question. "I don't know what I'll study yet. I'm a big science person, but I'm not sure where my focus would be."

"It's important to make goals, Iris. Know what you want," said Talbot's dad.

"Yeah, be sure and have a plan for everything and be bored the rest of your life," said Talbot. "That's our family's credo."

"That's enough, Talbot," said her mother.

"What, aren't I entitled to my own crappy opinion?" asked Talbot, throwing her fork down.

"Enough!" yelled her dad. "You, young lady, can go to your room."

Once Talbot was upstairs, her dad apologized to me. "She's just been so difficult. I'm sorry about this."

We sat in awkward silence for the rest of the meal, including when the berry cobbler came out. I was happy not to have to make conversation. I didn't think I was very good at it anyway. After dinner I was allowed to go upstairs and found Talbot in her room, playing music and looking at a magazine.

"My parents are such jerks," she said.

"It's okay. Mine are, too." I felt weird making it seem as though Mom were still alive. But I didn't know how to get out of it now. I went on and on in elaborate detail about what awful things she had done to me in the past few months, mostly stolen from Sierra's former tirades. Talbot listened with a sympathetic ear.

"We'll be out of here soon enough," she said.

"Where do you want to go to college?" I asked.

"College? It's not for me. At least not right away. I'm taking a year off to travel across the U.S. I mean, there's so much to see and learn through experience instead of learning it in a classroom."

"That's so cool that your parents are letting you do that!" I was jealous of her freedom.

"Well, they don't know about that plan yet," said Talbot.

"Oh."

"But what can they do? I'll be eighteen—a full-on adult. Then they won't have control over me anymore," she said.

I imagined, just for a second, what it would be like to ditch my Brown University plans and hop in a loaded car with Talbot, cruising the highways, meeting people from all over the globe, living a very different kind of life.

"Kevin is so hot," said Talbot, applying bright red lipstick at her vanity. When she finished, she leaned in toward the mirror and kissed her reflection—leaving a stain of lip marks.

"Who?" I asked.

"Kevin. Dog trainer Kevin."

"Oh, yeah." He was good looking, in a stereotypical Santa Cruz surfer kind of way.

"I bet he gets a lot of girls," Talbot said, wiping the lipstick off her lips and replacing it with a frosty pink hue.

"Maybe." I hadn't really given it much thought.

"Do you think he could be into me?" she asked.

Was she serious? "Talbot! You're like ten years younger than him. That's illegal!"

"First of all, I bet we're only around seven years younger than him, and besides, it's not like it would be the first time."

"What do you mean?" I asked.

"I mean, older men. Forget lame high school boys. I'm talking about a *real man*," she said, moving on to a dark eyeliner.

"You've done that?"

Talbot got up and locked her bedroom door and cranked up her stereo. "I had to promise I'd never talk about it again. As if *they* can control the words that come out of my mouth." Talbot rolled her eyes. "So last year, I was totally hooking up with my science teacher, Mr. Ettinger."

"Was it serious?" I asked.

Talbot nodded her head. "Very."

"So what happened?"

"We got caught."

"No." I couldn't believe what I was hearing. "Who caught you?"

"Stupid senior girls. They all had crushes on him. They were just jealous that he was giving me all his attention. They claimed they had questions about some science assignment. I figured he had locked the office door behind him, but then all of a sudden, those senior girls were there. They walked in on us kissing. They must have stolen the key from the receptionist. They totally sabotaged me."

"Did you get in trouble?" I asked.

"By the school? No way. In their eyes I was the victim of the whole situation. Poor, ignorant underage girl being seduced by the predatory science teacher. Mr. Ettinger was fired on the spot, and that was the end of that. The next thing I know I'm thrown into some weekly counseling group, and some woman named Ms. June is my new science teacher."

"Did your folks freak out?" I asked.

"They were such jerks. They pressed charges, and I guess Christopher is doing time somewhere in San Jose."

"Christopher?"

"Mr. Ettinger. He's not allowed to come within three hundred feet of a school of any kind. And he's never allowed to have contact with me again. I'm still mad at them."

"So the dog rehab isn't related to that?" I asked.

"It's completely related. I stole my parents' car. I had been at a party, and I'd had a few drinks, and then I just had to see Mr. E., but my parents called the car in as missing, and the cops were looking for it, and then I crashed on Highway 17 before I could even get to him.

My parents could have dropped the charges. I am their daughter. But they thought it would 'teach me a lesson.' All it taught me was that high school boys are way lame and Kevin is so hot!"

Would she think about her actions differently if she had known it was a drunk driver who had ended my mom's life?

I couldn't believe that after all she had been through she seemed willing to risk everything again. Kevin was cute and all, but he was our teacher, our superior, and I would never even have thought of crossing that line.

Talbot added some glittery eye shadow. "Whatever. Just one more school year and we're out of here, right?"

I shrugged.

"Sorry. I mean, I'm out of here. You'll be on your way to college, but at least you'll be out of high school. What's Santa Cruz High like?"

"Big," I said.

"You're lucky. At Clark, we only have fifty people per grade. I've been stuck with those same fifty people for the last six years. I can't stand it anymore."

"Yeah, but my school is so big, I kind of feel lost in it," I said.

"That's good, though. I'd love it if I could walk down the halls without someone knowing about what happened and calling me some awful name."

I didn't know how to tell her that sometimes I didn't want to be lost. In fact, it was just the opposite. Sometimes I wanted nothing more than for someone to reach out and find me.

"What's up with you and Sycamore?"

"Who?" I asked.

"Oak. I call him Sycamore. Sometimes I call him Redwood. Any tree will do. His parents must be total hippies. You are aware that he's totally into you."

Here I was wondering whether or not Oak's coffee proposition was romantic, and Talbot had him all figured out. She seemed to know a lot more about how to read a guy than I did.

"Well, he asked me to coffee," I said.

"That's a weird date activity."

"I'm kind of a caffeine addict," I explained.

"That means he's paying attention!" Talbot moved to her bed, and I followed. "So what did you say?"

"I told him I didn't have time," I said.

"Worst answer ever."

Talbot was right. What was I thinking? He'd never make that kind of effort again. I needed her expert opinion. "I was busy! What was I supposed to say?"

"You've got to give a guy something to hold on to. A promise of what's to come."

With all her experience with older men, it couldn't hurt me to heed her advice.

"So what should I do?" I asked.

She grabbed her phone. "You call him."

"I don't have his number," I told her, relieved.

"I do." Talbot removed a piece of paper from her bulletin board.

"Let me guess—you got his number from Kevin," I said, remembering that was where she got mine.

"Don't worry, I didn't just get his—I got the whole class. I'll dial." She began pressing buttons.

A rush of excitement and embarrassment ran through me.

She handed me the phone, which was already ringing on the other end.

"What do I say?" I panicked.

"Hello?" It was Oak.

Talbot was making kissing sounds, so I shooed her away.

"Hey. How's it going?" I asked.

"Who is this?"

"Oh, sorry." Why didn't he recognize my voice? "It's Iris...from dog rehab. I'm the one who has Roman."

"The Iris who has Roman. I'm glad you explained it to me that way because I know so many girls named Iris, I really can't keep track of them all."

I laughed. Okay, I guess I had gone a little far in qualifying who I was.

"What's up, Iris?"

"Nothing much. Um. Can you hold on a second?" I put the phone facedown into a pillow and looked over at Talbot.

"What's wrong?" she asked.

"I don't know what I'm supposed to say to him."

She grabbed the phone.

"What are you doing?" I whispered.

"I'll speak for you," she said.

I flashed back to reading the play *Cyrano de Bergerac* last year in Schneider's class. Things in the story went south quickly when Cyrano started speaking for Christian.

I grabbed the phone back. I might not have known what to say, but I certainly didn't want anyone else speaking for me.

"Hi, sorry about that," I said.

"What's going on over there?" asked Oak.

"Nothing. I'm at Talbot's. She's being difficult," I said, laughing.

"She's lying!" shouted Talbot.

"I've heard she's trouble," said Oak. I hoped he wasn't referring to the Mr. Ettinger incident. She was the victim in that situation, and it would really piss me off if he was claiming otherwise.

"Ask him to the bonfire next weekend," mouthed Talbot.

"What bonfire?" I mouthed back.

"Just ask him!" She egged me on.

"So, I was wondering…" How was I supposed to put this? "Do you like the beach?"

"Nah, breathtaking views kind of make me queasy," he said.

I had done it again. Why did I have to make myself look like a complete idiot?

"Yes, I like the beach, Iris with the dog named Roman," Oak said.

Here went nothing. "There's a bonfire next weekend, and I was wondering if you wanted to go."

Talbot gave me two thumbs up.

"Sure! Sounds great," said Oak.

That had been so easy!

I heard the sound of a car honking through the phone. "Hey, Iris. I gotta go. My car is blocking my dad in the driveway. But I'll see you on Monday."

"Okay. See you then."

"So?" asked Talbot when I had put the phone back on the charger.

"He's in," I said.

"Now there's just one thing," Talbot said.

"What's that?"

"We need to plan that bonfire."

I'd assumed when she told me to invite him to *the* bonfire that there was an actual bonfire to attend. "What are you talking about?"

Talbot opened her laptop and began typing an invitation over e-mail. Her recipient list was huge.

"Who are all those people?" I asked.

"Just a bunch of high schoolers from Harbor, SC, Kirby, Clark… people who know how to get the word out."

I couldn't believe she knew so many people.

"I just have to hit send and…" Talbot moved the cursor to *send* and clicked. "Consider the bonfire planned."

❀

Later, when it was time to go, I put my shoes back on, and her whole family walked me to the door.

"We hope you come back again soon!" said Talbot's mother.

Her father said to Talbot, "This friend is good for you."

Thaddeus shot me with his toy gun on the way out. I fired back with my finger.

I wheeled my bike outside and headed for Bay Street. I was looking forward to coasting downhill all the way home. In this moment, the waters within were ripple-free, like a glassy lake. Only the sound of my bike wheels spinning accompanied me home.

eight

I really didn't want to be the kind of girl who thought about boys all
the time. I wanted to rise above the tug and pull of attraction, but I
found myself constantly thinking about Oak. I even whipped out my
yearbook from the previous year and searched for him through the
pages. His class photo was missing, but I saw him in the background
of other pictures: In one, he was sitting in the library with his hood
covering his face; in another, he was wearing gym shorts and holding
a basketball with a hood over his face. I saw his frame, tall, lanky,
but I wanted to know more. Who was the boy beneath the hood?

It was the morning of Dad's promotional interview, and I could
tell he was nervous. He kept fidgeting with his new suit, rearranging
his tie, and checking his watch. Before I could tell him he looked nice
or wish him good luck, he was out the door, forgetting to pour the
coffee he had prepared, leaving me with the entire pot all for myself.

In class, Perry was wearing jeans and a T-shirt that read Reading
Is Sexy. Apparently, they eased up on the dress code over the summer,
even for teachers. I helped a few of the other kids with our morning
ritual of placing the chairs in a circle.

"Thanks!" Perry said.

Once we were all gathered, class began. A few of us had opened our notebooks, pens poised between fingers, when Perry interrupted. "Why don't you put the pens down?"

We all complied.

Perry circled the room. "I find it's much easier to really engage in a conversation if you aren't worried about writing everything down and you focus more on really listening."

A teacher who didn't want us to take notes? Another first for me—but then again, Perry definitely had her own way of doing things.

Once our notebooks and pens were out of service, Perry continued, "What do you think of when I say *fairy tales*?"

A few hands cropped up, none of them mine.

"Don't worry about hand-raising either. Just pretend you're in a real conversation." She paused and stared off into space for a second. She had a habit of getting lost in her own thoughts. Did I look the same when I did that?

"Scratch that," Perry said. "Don't *pretend*. Just *be* in a real conversation."

"Bedtime," said a girl from the softball team.

"Good versus evil," said one of the guys.

"Happily ever after?" I half-answered, half-asked.

Perry walked to the front of the class. "These are all great ideas. Keep 'em coming."

"Unfulfilled desire," said another girl, a theater geek.

Perry furiously scribbled everyone's ideas on the whiteboard.

Monsters, forests, not reality—the list continued. Perry practically danced around the room in excitement as answers flew out of our mouths faster and faster.

"This is all so excellent! What if I added 'sexual awakening'? What would you say?" asked Perry.

"I'd say it sounds good to me!" Roy Jones bellowed from across the circle. Everyone laughed.

The girl next to me, one of the students who had been ready with her pen, looked perplexed. Perry noticed right away.

"What's on your mind, Alexa?" Perry asked.

"It just seems to me that pushing some sort of sexual agenda onto stories meant for kids is…well, just kind of out there."

Perry took her point seriously. "Interesting and valid response. Fair enough. Some people ascribe to the notion that fairy tales were written for kids as a means of exposing them to, and letting them work through, their deepest fears. But there are other theories as well. What if I told you that a theory stands that fairy tales were not intended for young children but were actually meant to regulate young adults such as yourself?"

"You mean, fairy tales were like old-school sex ed?" asked Roy.

"Exactly!" Perry said, pointing at Roy.

"Can you be more specific?" asked Alexa, eyeing the pen she had left on her desk as though she wanted so desperately to pick it up and write all of this down.

Perry was right—when you stopped taking notes and focused on really listening, things changed. Not that I was saying much in this conversation, but I was still equally a part of it, just by being there.

"Let's look at Cinderella. We all know that one, right?" asked Perry.

Everyone nodded. Who didn't know the story of Cinderella?

Perry took a seat on top of her desk. "Bruno Bettelheim, who subscribed to Freud's theories of sexuality, believed that a story like this was a metaphor for sexual awakening. So in this story, can you guess what represented Cinderella's sexuality?"

"The pumpkin?" I offered, turning a bit red.

"Good guess. I'll give you a clue; it's something she loses."

"The glass slipper!" Most of us shouted out at the same time.

I couldn't believe I was being encouraged to talk about literature and sex in English class.

"So, according to Bettelheim, the glass slipper is Cinderella's lost virginity, never to return. A caution to girls everywhere to..." Perry's voice trailed off as she waited for a response.

"Never lose their shoes!" said Roy.

"Metaphorically speaking." Perry winked. "So, those of you eager to pull out those pens will be happy to know that now I'd like you all to get out a piece of paper and, through the use of any familiar fairy tale you'd like, brainstorm about what you think Bettelheim would say about the story in relation to a young woman's sexuality."

I was still in shock that this was summer school. Perry didn't want regurgitated facts. She wanted our ideas. I immediately began scanning my brain for fairy tales I knew. Were there any others about young women who lost something? Then my thoughts turned to my mom, who always had to wake me for school before I knew how to operate my alarm clock. She'd crawl into bed with me and run her fingers through my hair, saying the same thing every morning: "Wake up, Sleeping Beauty. It's time to greet the world."

Something I hadn't been eager to do in a very long time.

❁

By the time the bell rang, I had written six pages about how the needle of the sewing machine that Sleeping Beauty pricked her finger on represented some sort of phallic symbol, and her punishment for daring to be curious was falling into a never-ending sleep. I didn't know if this was right or if it was even what Perry wanted. But it felt good to be here in this moment, without distraction. Maybe I did understand why Kevin kept comparing me to Roman. Could it be that Roman and I had both become too tangled in our histories when all we really had was the moment before us?

Perry handed out a list of fairy tales, and our homework was to revise what we had worked on in class as well as pick an additional story to analyze at home. When Perry gave instructions, not one student groaned. As I scanned the various fairy tales I had grown up with, I wondered: Where in the world were all these girls' mothers?

❊

At home, on a whim, I decided to call Ashley. It had been nagging at me—seeing her in front of Pergolesi the other day without so much as an acknowledgment of my existence. Maybe I could just work it all out with a conversation. When I tried her home line, her mom picked up.

"Iris, Ashley isn't home right now," she said, although I could clearly hear Ashley singing in the background.

"Okay, just tell her I called," I said.

I couldn't believe she had refused to speak to me.

Moments later, my cell phone chimed. It was a text from Ashley. *I'm so sorry…my mom is…scared of you. She just needs some time to cool down. Promise.*

❊

"I nailed it!" said Dad when he poked his head into my room later that night. It was after ten, and I was already in bed.

"Congratulations," I said.

"Big things are gonna be happening around here, Iris! You'll have your new bike by the end of summer!"

His last declaration got me excited.

"Then maybe we can go for a big ride...maybe down to Monterey for a week," said Dad. He knew that I'd like nothing more than to take a biking vacation—to the world's best aquarium, no less.

"That would be awesome!" I said, feeling a sudden closeness to my dad. "When do you find out about the job?"

"A week or two. They have a couple of other candidates. Rick assured me it's just part of the process. They have to look like they gave everyone interested a fair shot."

I fell asleep that night thinking about my new bike and our trip to Monterey. I was so entrenched in my fantasy world that I hardly noticed the neighbor's dog, howling to be let in.

✿

I worked my way through Perry's class all week, analyzing Anne Sexton's poem "Rumpelstiltskin" and working on a small group project in which we had to write a rap from a fairy tale character's point of view. Luckily, Roy volunteered to present it to the class. He began beatboxing into his hands before rapping: "I'm big and green and kinda tall/If you climb up my beanstalk, you know you're gonna fall."

The class loved it.

Perry talked a lot about how various fairy tales had gone through many different incarnations. Cinderella could be traced all the way back to Roman times. In a Chinese version of the story, the girl's mother comes back as a fish whose bones have magical properties. And it wasn't until Charles Perrault's version that the pumpkin and glass slipper were added.

"Just like each of you are all unique, these stories have taken on different personalities," said Perry, handing out yet another assignment to complete.

I liked this idea of taking something and making it my own. It kind of reminded me of genetic mutations. You get a copy of something, but it's not an exact copy. But you still have the essence of what was once there. I hadn't seen the relationship between English and science before, but now I realized they could be linked. A biological cell was like a word. Molecules were like sentences. And bodies were like the essays made up of millions of cells.

Which reminded me I had a ten-page paper looming in my future. But before I could worry about that assignment, Perry launched into our next task.

"It's a fun assignment," she assured us. "And it involves a field trip." I hoped it wouldn't be too far, considering my only transportation was a bicycle.

"Instead of coming to school tomorrow, we're going to meet at Central Branch on Church."

A library. The absolute last place I wanted to be.

Perry continued, "I've broken you up into small groups meeting at various times throughout the day. I'll be there all day to help. I've already informed the librarians you'll be coming, and they will be ready to assist you. From this list, I'll ask you to focus on one of these writers. What do they all have in common? They've each rewritten fairy tales. Or reinterpreted them—putting their own spin on a classic. The ways in which they've rewritten the tales change their meaning completely and put them in a cultural context, reflecting concerns of society."

Her words began to melt together, and all I could focus on was the fact that tomorrow I'd be in a library. My mom's domain. Yet another place I'd been avoiding. I tried to distract myself by thinking about how I'd soon be at a bonfire with Oak. I couldn't tell which I felt more strongly about...terrified about the library or elated about the bonfire.

nine

As I approached the entrance to Central Branch Library, I thought about what Doug, my counselor, had said during our last session: It was okay for me to feel angry. Anger wasn't my enemy, but I had to take control over the way I dealt with it. I tried my best to let all of the emotions flooding my system—anger, anxiety, sorrow—wash over me like a wave as I entered the building.

But inside, the familiar mustiness overwhelmed me. It amazed me how the smell of stale books could make all of the mental preparation I had done completely disappear. I was living proof of an olfactory phenomenon I had only read about in my science books. It all came down to my emotional brain. Scientists were studying whether or not other animals possessed the ability to recall emotions via smell. As the scent traveled up my nostrils to my head, my palms grew sweaty and I froze—a prisoner of my own memory.

"Everything I'm feeling is okay," I reminded myself, plagiarizing from an affirmation Doug had repeated during each session, and I headed toward the computers. I remembered that when I was little they'd still used the old-fashioned card catalogues—large wooden pieces of furniture with rows and rows of mini-drawers filled with little three-by-five cards that listed each book alphabetically by author.

Computers made things a lot easier, but Mom would always talk about the glory days of the card catalogue. When her own library went digital, she lobbied to take one of the empty files home, and she placed it in our entryway. Over the years, we filled it with all sorts of knickknacks—items found at the beach or on our walks through Topanga: a bird's nest in one, seashells in another. It was her personal treasure trove.

What had happened to that piece? Had Dad just up and sold it when we moved without even consulting me? Yet another way he was showing me he totally didn't care—that my opinions didn't count.

Sitting at the new and improved computer catalogue system, I typed *fairy tales*, which directed me toward shelves upon shelves of books. The Brothers Grimm, Hans Christian Andersen—they were all there, altered versions of the same story told over and over again, just as Perry had explained. I thought about Perry's instruction to have us look at these stories differently, from an original point of view, in order to glean something new from the story. I liked that idea.

"Hey, Iris!" It was Bettina from my class. She had just arrived with Lorrie, the one who had refused to sit next to me on the first day of summer school.

A librarian emerged and immediately brought a finger to her lips, shushing the offending shouter. Lorrie had spotted other classmates, who waved us over to their corner table. I approached cautiously, a little on edge, taking in the library environment and trying not to think too much about my mom.

"Hey," I said, taking a seat. "What are you guys doing?"

"We were talking about the fact that the summer school crowd is unequivocally hotter than the non-summer schoolers," said a girl from class.

Now there was a mangled theory.

"I totally agree," said Bettina. "Delinquents are just better looking."

I was glad that I wasn't the only one who considered herself a delinquent.

"And we're also talking about the assignment," said Perry, who sat down with a pile of books that she fanned across the table. "I've played matchmaker here, trying to pair you up with texts that I think you'll get the most from." She handed out various books to people around the table, doling out the Brothers Grimm, Charles Perrault, Aesop, and John Francis Campbell. Soon everyone had a book but me.

"This is it." Perry passed the book to me, and I held it in my hands. "*The Bloody Chamber* by Angela Carter. She'll help you get an A."

"I'd pass the class with a C-minus," I said.

"Better to at least try for that A."

I scanned the cover. It gave me the creeps. Rapunzel was in her tower, screaming her head off. The tower was resting on what looked like an ocean of blood. The whole scene was kind of disturbing. I tried to imagine how this book could help me do anything but have nightmares.

"Take the next little while to read around your books," Perry instructed. "And then make some predictions on paper about how your particular author might interpret fairy tales. What kind of spin have they put on them?"

For the next thirty minutes, I was what my court-appointed therapist would refer to as a "healthy griever." I was going about my business in a place that reminded me of my mom on a sensory level, and I was surviving. This was a big deal.

But when Perry left our table to seek out some "lit crit," as she called it, the conversation turned.

"I'm so tired. I was hanging out on Pacific. I didn't get home until two," said Bettina.

"What were you doing?" asked Lorrie.

"My brother snuck me into the Catalyst to see Modest Mouse. It was awesome!" said Bettina. "What did you do last night, Iris?"

Summer break. Sixteen years old. Surely I could come up with something other than hammering a wall and watching nature shows. But before I could fabricate a fabulous Thursday night, Lorrie interrupted. "Beat anyone up lately?"

The group looked at her, stunned that she would let anything like this slip.

I had been doing my best just to fit in—go by unnoticed. That was it. I slammed my backpack down on the table. The noise it made was amplified by the fact that the library had been so quiet.

I got in Lorrie's face, as close as I could. I could feel her breath exiting her mouth.

"You really want to find out what I can do?" In that moment I felt as though I could have ripped her face off.

Before I could say anything more, Perry ran over and held both of my shoulders. I aggressively shrugged her off. "Don't touch me!" I yelled.

"Let's go outside," she said.

"Aren't there rules about this?" Lorrie asked.

Before I knew it, I was outside, my chest heaving in and out, a tightness taking hold in my throat.

"Just breathe," Perry said.

Part of me wanted to push her away. I was good at doing that. But instead, I went with my instinct and moved toward her, just a bit. It was enough to get her to move closer to me, arms open. And there we stood, her arms wrapped around me tightly, and she made a slight shushing in my ear while I cried with such force, I thought I would never be able to stop.

And then that moment passed, like a paper bag that had gotten caught in a temporary gust of wind before landing once again on the ground.

"Lorrie is just a bully. You can't let someone like that take control over you," said Perry.

"Why do you care what I do?" I asked.

"It's my job," she said.

I thought about other teachers at Santa Cruz High who didn't take their jobs seriously—teachers like Schneider who thrived on students' public humiliation. And others, like Ms. Kaminsky, who had always been too busy to talk to me. If only they all had the same standards as Perry.

Perry handed me a tissue. "How did you end up here?"

"I failed English." She must have known that already.

"I know, but I mean here in Santa Cruz. At this school?"

I told her the whole story, sparing few details. I didn't try to protect her from my grief or the tragedy of the situation.

Perry listened thoughtfully. "I don't know your dad, but why did you let him take you away?"

"What do you mean?" I asked, even though I fully understood.

"It sounds like he made you run away from everything you knew. Everyone you loved. It's hard enough to have a parent die. He didn't have to kill your whole world."

I'd spent so long making excuses for my dad, I'd neglected my own entitlement to happiness. He was the adult. It was *his* idea to move.

Maybe Perry was right. Maybe things wouldn't have turned out so awful if I had stayed in LA, at my school, with my friends, at our house, with miles and miles of beaches. I had spent so much energy being angry that I didn't even take the time to figure out what in the world I had been angry about. And yet Perry was able to articulate it so easily.

"It's just not fair," I said. That's how life was sometimes.

"I'll go back inside and grab your backpack for you, and then you can take off early."

I accepted Perry's kindness.

❧

My route home took me past Pergolesi again. The smell of roasting coffee made me circle around the block to do a drive-by to see if Ashley was there. No sign of her. I could safely get a cup of coffee without another confrontation.

It felt good to be in my favorite coffee shop again. But as I waited in line, Ashley emerged behind the counter, tying an apron to her back.

"Can I help you?" she asked before looking up.

"I'll have a latte, please," I said.

She recognized my voice right away, and our eyes met.

"Hey," she said.

"What's up? Actually, can you make it a double shot? I've kind of had a rough day," I said.

I was relieved that we weren't making lame small talk with each other; instead, I watched in silence as she retrieved my drink. But at the same time, I wanted more of an interaction. I wanted something real to pass between us.

As I went to pay, she put her hand up. "It's on the house," she said. She was about to say something more, but just then a gaggle of moms pushing their babies in strollers descended upon the counter, and I just waved good-bye and headed toward my bike.

I chugged the double latte as I cycled to dog training. By the time I got there, I was jittery, and I felt as though Roman could sense the change in my demeanor. He eyed me inquisitively.

"It's just me on caffeine, boy," I said, extending my hand out to him. When he pranced toward it, I didn't recoil. The coffee had made me brazen, or maybe it was something else. Maybe when I released all my emotions with Perry, I released some fear as well. I didn't want people to be afraid of me. I didn't want to be afraid of Roman. What if I met him with the same openness that Perry showed me?

Roman approached my hand and gave it a gentle nudge with his perpetually wet nose.

"Good boy," I said.

As we went through our routine of commands—sit, walk, stay, down, heel—I allowed Roman to touch my palm with his nose every time he successfully listened. This was what he had been trying to do for a while now. It was his way of saying, "I hear you." It felt good to be heard.

We moved on to a new command, *come*, which involved getting the dog to sit and stay as we walked a few paces away and then said, "Come," at which point the dog was supposed to bound toward us and resume a sitting position. But Roman was having a hard time with this one.

"You were doing so well, boy! Of all the days to be difficult," I said to him, "why are you picking today?"

I set Roman up with a *sit* and *stay*, and once again I moved away before calling for him. He just sat there, ears perked, staring at me. When I walked over to talk to him, he tried to nudge my palm with his nose.

"No," I said. "You need to do it right."

Kevin saw I was struggling and came over to give Roman some tougher leash corrections. Roman was acting like a horse about to buck its rider off.

"You excited for the bonfire tonight?" asked Talbot as we moved on to a new task: newspaper retrieval.

"If I can get through this afternoon," I said.

Oak smiled at me from across the lawn.

"Look!" said Randy. "I got Tinkerbelle to pick up a newspaper!" His little Chihuahua had managed to envelop an entire section of the paper in her mouth.

"Hope you perfected your 'come' command first—the newspaper trick was a bonus," said Kevin, still correcting Roman.

"Who in the world would want their dog to get them the newspaper?" asked Shelley.

"You'd be surprised at what little details are the make or break for potential dog adopters," said Kevin, who finally had gotten Roman to listen to the "come" command. "This retrieval talent has won over many a new owner."

Kevin handed me Roman's leash. "I'd go back to basics with him for today. Do the 'stay' command a few times before moving on to something new."

I got Roman to sit, but when it came time to stay, he fussed, standing up again the second I took a few steps back from him.

"Come on! Stay!" I shouted. This was a dog who knew how to do this but was choosing not to. We'd started the day so well, but now he was getting on my last nerve. My caffeine buzz was fading.

I walked over to him and did a harsher leash correction, the way I had seen Kevin do before. Roman growled and then lashed out at me, jumping off his one hind leg to try to bite my arm. Luckily, I saw it coming and quickly moved my arm out of harm's way. I was shaking with fear.

Today was not the day to mess with me.

"You okay, Iris?" shouted Kevin from across the lawn, working with Persia on the paper-retrieval technique.

"No!" I shouted back.

"What do you need?" he asked.

"I don't feel safe," I said.

It was as though I had said the four golden words. Right away, Kevin was at my side, taking command of Roman's leash.

"I'll see what I can do," he said, disappointed. "Just sit over here and watch until class is over. You don't need to work with him anymore."

I had a seat in the shade of a cypress tree and watched the others practice the exercise.

"Where is he taking Roman?" asked Talbot.

I just shrugged. Roman had scared me—that wasn't an exaggeration. As Kevin led him away from us, the dog let out a mournful cry that landed in the pit of my stomach.

How in the world was someone as damaged as me supposed to be able to help a dog like Roman?

ten

My closet wall reflected the terrible week I'd been having. I was running out of space to bash and was forced to branch out to the side walls of my closet, but it was cramped and hard to get a direct hit.

I had been looking forward to the bonfire all week, but now I just felt exhausted and deflated. I was a bad student, a bad dog trainer, and a bad friend.

Earlier in the evening, our neighbor with the dog had knocked on our front door. Thank God Dad hadn't been home because she had come over to inquire about the construction we were doing.

"There's no construction," I had said.

"Then what was all that hammering?"

I realized she was referring to my closet aggression. "Oh, that, yeah. We're putting up a photo wall," I lied.

"So it's done now?" she asked. "I was trying to nap."

I wanted to ask her how she was able to nap with her dog barking all the time, but instead I just said, "Yeah, pretty much done."

Talbot had been texting all afternoon, asking if she could come over first to my place so that we could walk down to the beach together. I ignored her because I didn't want her to come over and figure out that I didn't have a mother. She left me a long message saying I had better look cute. I didn't even know what that meant. Ashley and Sierra would have known exactly what to wear. Sierra had a flair for the dramatic (think corduroy bellbottoms and sequined headbands), and Ashley just understood fashion—which jeans fit which body type and what colors were in for each season.

My closet consisted mostly of ratty jeans and even rattier T-shirts, but I pulled the most respectable of each from the lot and culled together some semblance of a wannabe cute outfit. Jeans, black V-neck shirt, and a fuzzy orange sweater I'd bought on Front Street at a secondhand store the previous year.

"You kind of look like a bonfire," said Talbot when I found her on the beach, drinking out of a water bottle that had been refilled with beer.

Not quite the look I was going for.

"When's Oak coming?" she asked.

"We're meeting in five minutes at the trash cans by the volleyball courts."

"Trash cans...how romantic," said Talbot, apparently determined to make fun of every decision I made tonight.

She introduced me to a few people, some from Clark and some from Santa Cruz High—more students I hadn't even seen before.

There were about eighty kids so far, gathered in various groupings along the coastline. Santa Cruz had so many cool little beaches, I was surprised Talbot had chosen this one, but as the people poured in, I realized this beach, adjacent to the touristy Boardwalk, might possibly be the only one large enough to accommodate the growing crowd.

As I scanned the expanding mass of high schoolers (and a few local kids who hadn't done much but surf since graduating high school) I was surprised to see two familiar faces: Ashley and Sierra, who had their shoes off and their feet in the water.

It couldn't hurt to say hi.

"I'll be right back," I told Talbot and headed toward the ocean.

"Hey!" I said, walking close to the water's edge, trying to avoid getting my shoes wet.

The two of them turned around and registered that it was me, their troubled friend. They eyed each other, not sure what to do.

"Hey, Iris." Ashley was the first to speak. Her voice was gentle and inviting.

"How's your summer going?" I asked. It felt weird to be making small talk with people I once considered to be close friends.

"So fun!" said Sierra. "I move out to the dorms in a month! I've just been running around like a crazy person trying to get everything organized."

"She bought every gadget known to man," said Ashley.

"I did not," protested Sierra, eyes focused on the wet sand, not quite ready to make eye contact with me.

"What college student needs an espresso machine, a popcorn popper, and a bread maker?" asked Ashley.

"Oh my God, you guys, look," said Sierra, pointing up the beach toward the volleyball courts. We all turned around. "It's Hoodie Boy!"

I smiled, excited to see him, knowing he was there to meet me.

"He's such a freak!" said Sierra, flipping her head so that her hair whipped in front of her face and then putting her sweatshirt hood over her head, mimicking him.

Ashley laughed before pulling her own sweatshirt above her head.

This was my chance to get their friendship back. All I had to do was join them in their teasing, and they'd accept me.

I couldn't bring myself to do it.

"His name is Oak," I said and walked away from them, toward

the trash cans by the volleyball net, not even turning around to look at what I know must have been astonishment on their faces when I approached him. He and I hugged for a long time, then pulled away from each other, and he kissed me on my cheek.

"That was a nice welcome," said Oak. "Have you been here long?"

"Ten minutes, maybe? I ran into some old friends from school," I said, waving over to the girls, who were standing there dumbfounded, staring at me.

"Looks like this is gonna be huge," said Oak. "I got like twelve texts about it. I bet all of Santa Cruz High will be here."

That would be my absolute worst nightmare.

I tried to be in the moment with Oak, but my mind kept wandering to all of the potential run-ins I could have here tonight—all of the possible glares from fellow classmates.

"You look nice," Oak said, and I stopped worrying. "Do you go to lots of bonfires?"

"Yeah," I lied. Truth was, I'd seen them plenty of times from afar, but I had felt too intimidated to join in.

A small group gathered with their guitars and drums in a circle on the sand. Others were taking turns going into the center and dancing.

Oak took my hand and led me down the beach, away from the crowds, and we sat down in the sand.

"Don't you think it's kind of funny? You and I both made the dean's list last year, and now here we are, working for dog rehab," he said.

I had no idea Oak had also been on the dean's list. As I tried to remember the other students' names etched on that plaque, I vaguely recalled seeing his name on it and wondering who in the world that was.

"Oh, wow! That was you?" I said. "I didn't realize...so what colleges are you applying to?" I took off my shoes and dug my toes into the sand.

"I'm not going," he said, leaning back onto his elbows.

"Yeah, right," I retorted. "Dean's list and you're not applying to college." It sounded ridiculous—the kind of thing you say to parents when they piss you off enough to really scare them. The kind of thing Talbot would say.

Oak sat back up, serious. "Not everyone has to have a degree to be successful," he said. "I know what I'm good at—computers. I'm better at programming than most professional adults. I'm so good, in fact, that the Feds thought I was an entire ring of computer geniuses. After that whole thing went down, I was invited on a talk show in LA, but I said, 'No way!' I'm not going to be anyone's puppet. I'm ready to start my own life, Iris."

I never thought about things that way. I had been on a specific path my whole life, a path that I thought was unchangeable—go to high school, then Brown. It was just a given for me.

"But don't you want to have that college experience?" I asked, thinking about how many hours I'd spent with the girls talking about what college would be like—how we'd decorate our dorm rooms, the kind of guys we'd meet, how good it would feel to take charge of our own lives.

"What, getting drunk and cramming for more exams? Count me out," said Oak. "Besides, I already have my independence; I live in our back house. My parents never even go out there. They totally respect my space. What about you? Do your parents give you space? Or are they always on top of you?"

It would be so easy to lie to him, like I had with Talbot. That way I wouldn't have to answer any questions. He wouldn't have to look at me with sad eyes.

"It's just my dad. My mom died about two years ago."

"That sucks," he said. It was the perfect reaction.

I smiled. "Yeah, it totally sucks."

"How did she die? If you don't mind me asking."

"Drunk driver," I said, looking over at Talbot dancing wildly in the center of the drum circle, her beer-filled water bottle in her hand. In another world it could have been Talbot who had been behind the wheel the night my mom died. I tried to shake that thought—tried to separate my new friend from the girl who got busted for driving drunk. But it wasn't easy.

Oak didn't barrage me with a million questions. He didn't try to comfort me. We sat there quietly for a moment, and then he changed the subject.

"So when do you get your new dog?" he asked.

I had been so distracted by the library incident and then getting ready for the bonfire that I hadn't thought about Roman. But when Kevin had said I wouldn't be working with him anymore, I instantly regretted opening my big mouth. Roman had scared me, but I didn't want to completely give up on him.

"I don't know. I feel bad, like I cried wolf or something. Kevin took it so seriously."

"He had to. You have to feel safe with your dog," said Oak.

"I did. I do, it's just, sometimes I don't think I'm the best match for that dog. It's like he has too much going on in his head."

Oak put his hand on top of my own head and began jostling it around. "Sounds like someone else I know."

Maybe he was right. Maybe I was the perfect person to help Roman, and I had just abandoned my duty. I had to get him back. I hoped Kevin would understand that Roman had caught me in a moment of weakness. But I'd be stronger. I just hoped it wasn't too late.

Oak and I had both become transfixed by the crashing of the waves—the rhythm of the tidal pull. Oak scooted his body closer to me until I could feel the heat emanating between our faces. I turned to look at him, and he did the same, both of us reveling in the moment right before a first kiss.

Then he leaned toward me and pressed his lips to mine. They were salty from the ocean air. Everything was perfect.

I caught a glimpse of Talbot, taking another turn in the drum circle. She flung her hair all around and shimmied, waving her arms freely up in the air. In the middle of her twirling, Talbot caught sight of us in the sand and came running over. She nestled herself between the two of us and, putting her arms around our shoulders, pulled us in close.

"Hello, my little lovebirds."

I was going to kill her.

"What's up?" I said.

Talbot pulled a beer out of her jacket pocket and refilled her water bottle. "Want one?"

I shook my head no.

"How about you, Oak?"

"Thanks, but I can't afford to get into any more trouble."

"Yeah, I know what you mean," said Talbot, tipping her head back and guzzling.

The sun had completely set, and the bonfire grew and glowed from across the beach. There was something magical about hearing the waves in the background and seeing people's faces lit up by the flames of the bonfire.

I couldn't think of another person I'd rather share this night with than Oak.

But just when I thought that the night would be nothing but successful, a jerk from Santa Cruz High, who had obviously been drinking, ambled toward me and shouted, "Hey! It's the psycho from school!"

I hadn't been prepared for this type of assault. *The waters rose fast and furious*; I could practically taste my rage rising through the back of my throat.

His screaming had attracted the attention of the crowd. I couldn't just let him call me out like that. Before I knew it, I was on my feet.

"You're a wild one, aren't you? Is she?" the guy asked Oak and winked, mistakenly thinking they were about to share some knowing fraternal gesture. He moved around me like a bullfighter taunting a bull. He had forgotten one small fact—that once in a while, the bull would lunge out and attack the fighter, stabbing him through the chest with his sharp horns.

"Iris, let's get out of here," said Oak, taking my hand and trying to lead me away from the tenuous situation.

"Let go of me," I said, throwing his hand from mine.

By now a large crowd had gathered, all staring at me, waiting to see what I would do. The taunter was still moving around me, waiting for me to pounce, waiting to see the beast in action, wanting to see proof of my reputation. If he came any closer, I would have no choice but to attack.

Oak put his hands on the perpetrator's shoulders. "That's enough, man," Oak said, trying to get him to stop.

I was angry with the guy, but now I was growing angry at Oak. Why did he feel as though he had to step in and rescue me? I could take care of myself. Once Oak had sent the guy on his way and the crowd dissipated, I walked away into the darkness, back toward my house.

It felt good to be alone. But it didn't last long.

"Iris! Wait up!"

I turned around. Oak was running toward me.

"Leave me alone," I shouted back. But he moved faster than me and was soon at my side.

The fog was filling the streets as though someone were standing there with a fog machine. The haze danced and swirled around streetlights.

"Iris, just let me talk. I was only trying to help you!"

I whipped around quickly. "I don't need your help! I'm fine on my own. I have been for a long time. You don't need to rescue me. I'm not some damsel in distress."

We were standing in the middle of my street, yelling at the top of our lungs. A few lights turned on in people's houses, but I didn't care. The neighbor's dog began to bark.

"Just please go home," I said and continued up to my house and walked through the door. The people on the bottom story of our duplex must have been visiting for the weekend because their lights turned on—their weekend of relaxation interrupted by an angry teen on the street who didn't know what she wanted.

Inside, as I got ready for bed, I thought about all of the stories we had reviewed in Perry's class—all of the women in fairy tales who needed to be saved.

I didn't want to be anything like them.

eleven

The funny thing about anger is that it sneaks up on you, and then suddenly you've reached full throttle. And then the feeling slowly slinks away until you feel normal again. When I awoke the next morning, I remembered how angry I had been the previous night, but connecting it to any one actual incident proved to be more difficult. It was as if the anger had been sitting there, pooling within, waiting to be released. It didn't really matter what triggered it.

I hadn't realized how much damage I'd done to my closet wall until that morning, when I had to pick up the pieces of plaster that had gathered on my carpet. I moved my clothing out of the way, revealing the entire wall of destruction. *How had I been capable of this?*

I spent the weekend holed up in my home, rotating between watching TV on the couch and making fresh pots of coffee. I thought maybe Oak would try to reach out to me, but my phone stayed radio silent.

On Monday morning, I turned on the TV to keep me company as I got dressed for an early morning therapy session. English class had been cancelled for the day due to personal reasons, and I had rescheduled my appointment for that morning. To my dismay, the cable was out, so I left Dad a note on the kitchen table.

Once I arrived at therapy, I decided that it was time to tell Doug about my closet wall.

"It's interesting how we choose to deal with our anger, isn't it?" he said, after I brought him up to speed on Friday night's hammering session.

"It's the best way I've found to deal with the problem. No one gets hurt," I said.

"But you're not really doing anything to deal with the issue," Doug said, much to my disappointment.

Here I was thinking that each time the hammer made contact with the wall, I'd avoided hurting someone.

"So what should I be doing, then?" I asked. He was, after all, the expert.

"Try talking to the direct source of conflict."

"It's that easy?"

"No. It's not easy. Not easy at all. But it works. And you'll feel a whole lot freer once you do it."

Doug spent the rest of the session sharing some confrontation strategies with me. I didn't know whether or not I was ready to use them. But they were good to keep in my proverbial back pocket, just in case.

At the end of the session, Doug walked me to the door. "And this concludes our last session."

"That's it?" I said. "I thought we were just getting started!" As much as I'd hated therapy at first, I'd come to rely on it.

"You've done great, Iris. But budget cuts dictate we don't have as much time as we'd like to counsel incarcerated teens."

My time was officially up for good.

❈

Not to say that I wasn't still annoyed at Oak for trying to be my knight in shining armor—it was the last thing I wanted—but when I saw him at dog training, I was ready to forgive him on the spot.

"Hey!" I said, mustering the biggest smile I could. I knew I had come down too hard on him. I'd reacted instead of thinking things through, as Doug would have suggested.

Oak barely waved, then turned his back toward me and struck up a conversation with Randy.

"You missed all the fun the other night," said Talbot, hiding behind wide-rimmed sunglasses. "That party was off the hook! The entire under-eighteen population was there! The cops finally broke it up at eleven, but then we just moved down to Lighthouse Field Beach. We did it all over again last night!"

"Iris!" said Kevin. He wasn't holding a new dog for me. In fact, there were absolutely no dogs present.

"Where are the mutts?" asked Randy.

"Let's gather over here," said Kevin, motioning us toward the shade of a cypress tree. It was an especially sunny day, and even though we were all wearing tank tops and shorts, I could feel the sweat dripping down the nape of my neck.

"I have an issue," Kevin said.

"We all have issues," said Talbot, rubbing her temples. She seemed to still be recovering.

"My van broke down last night," said Kevin. "I'm getting the battery replaced today, but I had no way of transporting all the dogs. And you," said Kevin, looking straight at me. "We'll have to come up with a completely different solution for your situation. We're looking for a new dog for you."

Although I was secretly relieved that I didn't have to deal with my discomfort working with Roman, I couldn't shake the nagging feeling that I had let both the dog and Kevin down.

"Thank God! We get the afternoon off!" cheered Talbot, flopping herself backwards on the grass.

"Not quite," said Kevin. He distributed our leashes.

"Um, but we have no dogs," said Oak. It was now perfectly clear he was avoiding all eye contact with me.

"Who says you need a dog to practice training techniques?" said Kevin, standing now, holding a leash, and pretending to walk an invisible dog.

"He has to be kidding," I said, observing how ridiculous Kevin looked.

"What command am I giving now?" Kevin shouted to us from across the grass. He tugged the leash upwards.

"Sit!" Randy and I yelled at the same time.

Talbot held her ears. "Can you guys whisper?" she asked.

"Sorry!" I mouthed.

"How about now?" Kevin asked, moving his extended arm down in a sweeping motion.

"Lie down!" yelled Oak.

"Seriously, you guys!" said Talbot, scooting herself away from the group.

Kevin ran back to us and told us to get our leashes.

"We're running through the whole shebang today—stay, sit, walk, lie down, newspaper retrieval, fetch, jump up, bark…" He seemed way too excited about making us look like complete idiots.

"Bark?" I asked. "Really?"

Randy laughed and started barking.

"Randy!" yelled Talbot.

So that's how we spent the afternoon, running around the grass, training invisible dogs on leashes. People who saw us probably thought we were visiting from a neighboring asylum, out for our daily breath of fresh air.

And the crooked smile on Kevin's face suggested that this wasn't so much an exercise in dog training as one in humility—which, by glancing at Oak, I was beginning to think could come in handy.

❁

When our session was over, Oak took off before I could speak with him. I guess being yelled at in public wasn't his thing. I didn't blame him for being upset, but I wished he could have at least given a girl a chance to explain herself.

"Wanna hit the beach?" asked Talbot. "I could go for a long nap on the sand."

"Sure," I said. It sounded pretty good, actually.

I left my bike locked near dog training, and we strolled to Natural Bridges, a big stretch of beach by Santa Cruz's standards.

"Don't you feel so lucky to live here?" said Talbot, always the optimist, laying out her towel on the sand. Not anticipating a beach trip, I hadn't come prepared and sat crossed-legged on my sweatshirt.

I didn't feel all that lucky about anything in my life.

Talbot took off her shirt and shorts, revealing a small turquoise bikini with green piping. She had more confidence than I'd ever have.

"So what's with Oak giving you the cold shoulder today?" she asked. I knew it would only be a matter of time before she brought it up.

"Was it that obvious?"

"Um, yeah, he's usually like all over you," she said.

"No, he's not."

"Well, at least with his eyes. He knows where you are at all times during dog rehab."

I had been so busy thinking about him that I'd failed to notice him thinking about me.

"We had a fight. Friday night. Didn't you see?"

Talbot nodded. "Yeah. I didn't think it was that big of a deal."

"It continued. After the beach, I mean. We fought in the street."

"How dramatic!" said Talbot, who seemed excited by the theatrics, whereas I was so embarrassed by the whole thing.

"I just don't want him to think he needs to help me," I said.

"I think it's nice to have a guy look out for you."

"Yeah, but I don't want help," I said.

"Okay, okay."

We sat there quietly, soaking in the sun's rays.

"Did you see the way everyone looked at me the other night? Like I was some sort of monster," I said under my breath.

Talbot sat up, took off her sunglasses, and looked straight at me.

"Hey! That was one jerk. You can't base everything on his stupid opinion. No one even likes that guy," she said, lying back down.

"Maybe I scared Oak away," I said.

"Um, I don't know if you've noticed, but the guy is kind of fearless."

That was exactly what I liked about him.

"You're so lucky. I wish I had some summer loving," Talbot said, eyeing three surfers exiting the water with their surfboards under their arms. "I got a letter from Mr. Ettinger."

I thought it was funny that she still called him that.

"From jail?" I asked.

Talbot nodded.

"But isn't he like banned from even thinking about you forever?"

Talbot was quietly contemplative for a moment. "He sent it to a friend of mine, from school. So it wouldn't be obvious it was to me."

"What did it say?"

"Just talked about jail. The food. His roommate."

"You're making it sound like college," I said.

"Well, to me, they're both a kind of prison, don't you think?"

I hadn't thought about college in those terms before. It didn't seem like a punishment to me, just the next stop in my educational path. But then I thought about how college wasn't even on the radar for Oak and how at this time next year, Talbot would be cruising the country's highways, going wherever she pleased.

"He says he misses me, and he's been thinking about me," Talbot said.

"Are you going to write back?" I asked.

"I have to figure out a way to do it. If they find out he's talking to me, he could get more time."

The afternoon heat was oppressive. Pools of sweat formed under my arms, at the back of my knees; even my palms seemed sweaty.

I looked out at the expansive ocean and watched as the waves hypnotized me into a reverie, taking me back to all those times I swam with my mom. Maybe I hadn't been completely lying when I told Talbot she was still alive. Life wasn't only about the physical being. If I could let those waves wash over me, maybe there was still a piece of her out there left behind for me.

"Wanna go for a swim?" I surprised myself with my own question.

"This is kind of embarrassing, but I'm scared of the ocean," said Talbot.

"Do you know how to swim?" I asked.

"In a chlorinated pool? Yes," said Talbot.

I couldn't believe what I was hearing. "*You're* afraid of something?"

"Is that so hard to believe?"

"You just seem so…full of adventure," I said.

"You don't worry about what's out there? The things you can't even see?"

My only fear of the water had to do with how I'd react after returning to it after so long. It wasn't what was out there—it was that it might remind me of what was missing right here.

"C'mon." I stood up and shook the sand off my legs. I'd been down to my black sports bra for options this morning—it would pass just fine as a bikini top. And if I swam in my shorts, they'd dry out pretty quickly in this heat.

"Where are we going?" Talbot asked.

I reached out for her hand.

"I am going to take you on a tour of the ocean."

Talbot hesitated. "The last time I attempted to go swimming, a huge wave crashed over me and filled my entire bathing suit with sand. I had to be rescued by a lifeguard. He was super cute, by the way, which was the only positive thing about the whole experience."

I continued to hold my hand out to my friend, and she took hold. We walked together toward the water's edge, getting our toes wet. Talbot followed me as I waded in past my waist, approaching the point where the waves were breaking.

"Those waves are so big!" shouted Talbot.

Returning to the ocean felt like coming home, as though I had been reunited with a part of myself I'd been missing. It completely invigorated me.

"I've swam in bigger!" I called back and dove under the crest of the next wave, feeling a tingle as the cold water washed through my hair, sending a shiver all the way down to my feet. When I surfaced, Talbot was treading water, trying to see below her.

"Where did you learn to swim like that?" she asked.

"My mom," I shouted above the crashing sound of the waves that were now behind us. "She was part fish."

I had spoken in the past tense, which meant I had given myself away. But Talbot hadn't seemed to notice.

This was my favorite space in the ocean—past the waves, where the water sloshed but wasn't violent. A place where I could forget I was even in an ocean. The place where Mom and I would have contests to see who could tread water the longest or who could swim out to the buoys and back the fastest. Once she put me up to the challenge of seeing who was brave enough to swim toward a passing pod of dolphins. Mom was everywhere in these waters, and my only regret was that it had taken two years to get back to her.

Talbot was too far away notice the tears streaming down my face.

"What the hell is that?" she screamed, looking down.

"Stop looking down!" I said.

"No, seriously, there's something down there!" She was panicking.

I swam over to her. She was awkwardly treading water, keeping her limbs in close, which made her movements more frantic and exhausting.

"Where?" I asked.

"There! It was right there. Oh my God. I think it's a shark. We're totally gonna die!"

I followed the direction of her pointing finger. Stillness. Nothingness. And then a dark shape swam under us and circled back. I had seen enough nature shows to know that sharks circle their prey before attacking. All we had to do was make it back to the waves and ride them in.

I tried to sound calm. "Maybe we *should* head back."

"Oh my God. It *is* a shark!" Talbot grabbed on to me, making it difficult to stay above water.

"Talbot! Chill out! Just follow me."

Again I looked down at the figure, getting larger, swimming closer to us. And before I could get either of us to move, it broke the surface of the water. Talbot screamed at the sight of the large seal's head bobbing along beside us. It stared at us and seemingly smiled, as though it had just pulled a practical joke on us.

"That's not a shark," Talbot said, relieved.

"Definitely not," I said. "It's just a seal."

"Do they bite?"

"Nah…not unless you're a fish."

A few scattered seal heads popped up, joining their friend to see what curious creatures had entered their space.

"Oh my God!" said Talbot. She had a look of wonder on her face, like a little kid.

"Do you still want to go back?" I asked.

"No way! This is amazing!"

Later, we rested on the beach until we were dried and sun-kissed, then headed back to our bikes.

"Thank you," Talbot said.

"For what?"

"For that," she said, gesturing toward the Pacific. "I can't wait to see what kind of reaction my dad has when I tell him I went so far out in the ocean."

"Maybe you shouldn't tell him?" I suggested.

"But it's such an incredibly rich opportunity to piss him off!"

As we rode our separate ways, I thought about how she was working so hard to cause friction with her dad while I was doing my best to mend the tension that was always present between my dad and me. Maybe Dad and I just needed to be more like those seals out there, more curious about each other, more willing to get to know that other strange creature living inside the house—more willing to play.

Maybe I didn't always have to feel as though I were sinking. Maybe it was okay to rely on others to keep me afloat.

twelve

The one good thing about the cable being out at our house was that I had no excuse to blow off my schoolwork. For the next week, I spent my afternoons reading Angela Carter at various coffee houses throughout the city. In her stories, women weren't helpless victims; they were fierce warriors in charge of their own destinies.

The first story, "The Bloody Chamber," ended with the main character's mother saving her from the wicked prince. I loved the departure from the stereotypical fairy tale endings, but I wondered who would rescue me now that my mother was gone.

I continued to leave Dad notes and texts about fixing the cable, and he responded with, "I'll get right on it." But he never did, which forced me to keep reading.

Carter's stories were fierce, feminist, and, at times, gory. It was the very last story in the collection, "Wolf-Alice," that really grabbed my attention. "Wolf-Alice" was based on the tale of Little Red Riding Hood, but in this version, nuns attempt to tame a feral girl. No one can understand what the girl is saying. She communicates by howling, which made me immediately think of Roman's mournful voice when Kevin last took him away. Thinking about the number of times I had been misunderstood over the past year, I further understood that

Roman and I weren't so different.

After the incident at the Central Branch Library, I'd decided that the University of Santa Cruz library was where I wanted to brainstorm ideas for my paper. The university handed out honorary library cards to SC High School students, so I was able to hitch my bike to the front of the 1 University bus that took me up the hill, past Talbot's house, toward campus.

The more time I spent up on the campus, the more I liked it—especially the science library. Unlike the regular library that everyone used, this one was filled with science buffs like me. In one corner, a couple nestled on a couch perusing a book on molecular science; at a round table, students discussed the effects of vanishing coral reefs and admonished the government's lack of interception on the matter. The library was alive with ideas, and I desperately wanted to be a part of it all.

But instead of a science book in my hand, I sat with the Carter book, hiding the cover of a girl shrieking from her tower. When I'd first seen the cover, I'd assumed the girl was calling out to be rescued. But now that I was on my second reading, I imagined the girl on the cover sounding a war cry, letting everyone within earshot know that it was time for her voice to be heard.

I liked everything in the Carter book, but I didn't know exactly what I was going to write about for my final paper. Perry had made it clear that we needed to have a specific argument, and I had to come up with it quickly because Perry wanted to see rough drafts before we turned in our final papers.

I decided a trip to my bench would do me some good. I could clear my head and figure out what in the world I was going to write for my final paper.

But once I got to my bench overlooking the ocean, I defaulted to list-making. One page was titled *Things to Do before I Die*, another was *Types of Juice I'd Include in My Hypothetical Juice Store*, and, finally, *Top Ten All-Time Best Movie Kisses*, which involved imagining me kissing Oak in each cinematic scenario.

I was just writing down my number-one all-time kiss movie, *Casablanca*, when I heard someone say, "Iris? You're on my bench!"

It was Kevin, wearing nothing but swim trunks. In his right arm he held a surfboard and in his left a wetsuit.

"What are you doing here?" I asked.

"This is the place I come…to think."

"Really?" But this was *my* bench.

"It's kind of been my place since back in high school. Maybe even earlier."

"I'm surprised we haven't run into each other here before," I said.

"Guess we think at different times."

I laughed.

"Mind if I have a seat?" he asked.

"Sure, it's your bench, too."

I moved over and made room for him. I got it now, what Talbot was going on and on about: Kevin cared. And I think that's what Talbot was confusing with attraction.

"You know, I was really disappointed with how everything went down at dog rehab," he said.

"Yeah—me, too." It was the truth.

Kevin slid his surfboard under the bench. "We were all in it together, and you kind of abandoned your dog."

"I didn't mean to. I mean, sometimes I feel like I don't even have a choice."

"Everyone always has a choice, Iris. You think you're the only one who gets angry? You know why I get to work in this program? Estelle, the woman who runs it, wanted someone who understood where these kinds of kids were coming from."

"You mean kids like me," I said.

"Yeah, kids like you. Angry kids. Kids who break the rules and pretend to not care what others think about them. So she picked me to be in charge because I can completely understand what it is you're going through."

"I seriously doubt that," I said.

"Look, my parents split when I was eleven years old. I hated both of them for it. Their fights were vicious. Dad used violence to solve his problems—I hated him for it, but I hated myself even more for doing the same thing to others. I stopped listening to my mom, stopped respecting any adult because I believed they were all full of it. I thought they only spoke in lies. I started getting into all sorts of trouble. Stealing, graffiti, drugs. You name it, I did it. But I crossed paths with a judge—a very sympathetic judge who had heard about this program called Ruff Rehabilitation."

"You went through the program?" I couldn't believe it.

"I didn't just go through it. I passed with flying colors. I had something to focus on other than my own misery. I turned things around. I liked the dogs, and the dogs liked me, and they listened. Since you guys have come to the program, have I ever once turned my back on you or told you that you couldn't do it?"

"No. Of course not," I said. Kevin had always been nothing but supportive.

"Then why did you turn your back on us? On Roman? He needs you, Iris, more than you'll ever understand."

The thought that a three-legged mutt needed me was almost laughable.

"I heard possible whispers that maybe you'd like Roman back?" said Kevin. Oak must have told him how I had been feeling.

"I think so," I said, sheepishly.

"You *think* so? Or you *know* so? Because you have to know so if you're gonna get him back." Kevin meant serious business.

"I think I know so," I said, still not completely sure that this was what I should be doing.

"Okay, then!" said Kevin. "I talked to Estelle last night. She made it very clear that I only get one free pass with her, but she says she'll break protocol and let you work with Roman. But you have to really be with the program, Iris. You have to trust the program."

There wasn't one person on earth that I did trust, and now Kevin was trying to convince me to trust an entire program.

"So, for the last time, are you in? I wouldn't be so insistent if I didn't believe in you so much, Iris. And Roman believes in you, too," said Kevin, picking up his surfboard.

"Can he talk now?" I asked.

"You'd be surprised at how much a dog can say without ever talking."

Here was this amazingly compassionate guy begging me to work with Roman again because he thought I could do it. How could I say no?

"I'll do it. But I can't promise I'll like it," I said.

"There's still hope, Iris. There's still hope." He put his hand out to mine, and I shook it. "See you on Monday? Don't be late." He picked up his wetsuit and started walking down the trail.

❋

Excitement replaced fear when Roman bounded toward me. His tail was wagging so enthusiastically against my bare legs that it felt like I was being whipped. He then proceeded to lick my entire face, and for the first time, I let him, with pleasure. For every lick, I reciprocated with a vigorous scratch behind his ears.

"Aw! He missed you!" said Talbot, watching us.

I knew I had made the right choice.

Oak pretty much avoided me during dog training. Would we ever talk again? I was playing a weird game of chicken with him. I didn't want to be the first to relent and speak. So I waited and waited, hoping to distract myself by chatting with Talbot.

"Girls, less talking, more walking!" Kevin shouted at us as we walked with our dogs in a circle, keeping the animals in a heel position to the left of our bodies. The tips of their noses had to stay behind our bodies at all times in order to ensure that the dogs knew who was boss.

"Sit and stay!" shouted Kevin. We were getting accustomed to these commands, so much so that it felt like we had all learned a different language. We each had our dogs sit in a row, leaving at least five feet between dogs and ten for Tinkerbelle, who was usually completely unfocused.

"Sit," I said. Roman went straight down.

"Good boy," I praised.

The others also gave the "sit" command, and down their dogs went. It was a sight to see these misfit dogs obeying our commands perfectly.

"They're all totally gonna find new homes!" said Talbot.

"I hope so," said Kevin.

"Stay," we said to our dogs, putting our hands out like we were making a stop sign. Then we slowly stepped backwards. When I felt like he was concentrating completely, I let go of Roman's leash. Roman didn't take his eyes off me. In my periphery I could see bicyclists going for an afternoon cycle along the beach. Birds were pecking at the ground, but Roman continued to zero in on me. Then a boy and his dad emerged with a bright red kite in tow. Roman started to lose his concentration.

"Stay!" I repeated sternly. He looked back at me, then toward the boy. I could see his internal struggle: listen or rebel.

Roman eyed the kite as the boy prepared it for takeoff.

"Stay!" I repeated sternly. Again Roman looked back at me, then back at the boy.

The dad ran with the kite and launched it into the air, where it floated on the wind currents like a seagull. But the duo was coming too close to us. Roman looked back at the kite. This was a total distraction for a dog like him. I knew that what he saw was an unidentified, jerkily moving object, the perfect thing to spook a sensitive dog like Roman, just like when my hand came down behind him that first week of dog training and I thought he was going to bite it off. I decided it was best to go back to where Roman was sitting and grab the leash so I could regain control.

Kevin nodded as though he were reading my mind as I made my way toward Roman, readying myself to grab the leash.

But then the kite erratically swooped over our heads. Every dog's head turned, following the kite, but Roman took off after it, ready to protect us all from the hovering beast. He barked and gnarled his way over to the kite, which finally landed at the base of a blooming purple jacaranda tree, right next to where the boy was standing.

"Sebastian!" yelled his dad, running full throttle over to the boy. I raced toward Roman. We were both running after our babies.

Sebastian's dad got there first, scooped up his son, and then began kicking Roman away.

"Don't do that!" I yelled. "He'll snap!" I knew that a foot flying toward Roman would be the one thing to trigger his aggressive past. Roman began growling and getting into an attack stance. Kevin was suddenly at my side, grabbing hold of the trailing leash.

"I'm so sorry about that, sir," said Kevin to the dad.

"It wasn't his fault!" I defended Roman. "He was protecting me from the kite."

"That dog tried to attack us," Sebastian's dad said.

"Why would you bring your kid out to play in the exact same spot where a group of dogs are being trained?" I asked, furious that Roman was even put in this situation. "You have the whole park!"

Kevin placed his hand on my shoulder. "Iris, I'm gonna ask that you go back and join the group now."

I had no choice but to listen. As I walked away, I heard the dad say, "Just so you know, I'm a lawyer. If something isn't done about that dog, get ready to see a lawsuit."

I couldn't believe this was happening. It all seemed so unfair. *The waters tossed and churned inside.* My anger swelled, and I could feel myself trying to ignore it, pretend it wasn't there. I thought about what my therapist had said: *Acknowledge it.* I started pacing around the trees. Weaving in and out of the dogs and their trainers. I must have looked like a nutcase. But in my head, I had to walk it off or else I would do something terrible.

Oak approached me. "Are you okay?"

Was he trying to save me again?

"I'm just checking in," he said, as though he knew exactly what I had been thinking.

At least he was talking to me. It meant he still cared.

Normally I would have said, "I'm fine." I would have sucked it all in. But now, I tried a new approach. "No, I'm not. I'm super pissed off. I need some space."

He didn't look hurt. He didn't look at me like I was crazy. Instead, he listened to my words and nodded as he went back to the group.

And then, as quickly as the anger had shot through me, the physical reaction started draining, like a water balloon with a leak, until I was left standing there, the same as before—still upset, but not out of control.

Kevin and the boy's father were done talking now, and Kevin was leading Roman back to his van.

"Where are you taking him?" I asked. I had a right to know where my dog was going.

"That boy's dad felt really threatened, and I don't blame him," said Kevin.

"But Roman wasn't going after him," I said.

Kevin looked so serious. "That's not how he saw it. If we get enough complaints, it will shut down the program. And what would that do to help these dogs?"

"So where is he going?" I asked again, desperately needing an answer.

"He needs some time to cool off. We can't work with a dog that has a complaint against him, and I guarantee you that man will file a complaint as soon as he gets home. Roman is in good hands, Iris. Don't worry."

That was an impossible request.

It was as though the minute I resolved to be there for Roman, he was taken away from me.

Before I knew it, Kevin had ushered Roman into the van. I didn't even get to say good-bye. I had gone from anger to sorrow in a matter of minutes.

This time, when Talbot came over to comfort me, I let her put her arms around me and hold me while I closed my eyes and let the sadness envelop me.

❀

At home I brought in a pile of mail consisting solely of bills. Many were in red envelopes. Red—the color of the kite that took Roman away. The color of anger. It was never a good color. I opened the water and power and gas bills, all of which were on their final notice before shutoff. Then I opened the cable bill and was reminded of what I already knew—the cable had been shut off. The problem was way bigger than me not being able to watch my animal shows. Our lives were being shut down. How could Dad have let this happen?

There must have been some sort of mistake. Even though Dad often got distracted by work, he never was one to be late on any sort of payment. He always used to joke with my mom that he even had a perfect library account—not one late fee.

I called him at work and, when prompted, hit his office extension. I heard a strange beep before the system hung up on me. I tried again. The same thing happened. I tried calling him on his cell, but it went straight to voice mail. After texting twice, I gave up, placed the envelopes in the middle of the breakfast table so he'd be sure and see them as soon as he got home, and continued working on my final paper.

I had decided to stick with the theme of missing mothers. I had a theory that they had to die in order for their daughters to find their own identity.

The thing was—this theory didn't apply to my situation, just fairy tales. I was without my mother and felt more lost than ever. I began feverishly brainstorming ideas, pausing only when the barking dog next door distracted me and my thoughts would momentarily turn to Roman.

When would I see him again? Did he miss me? I felt like I was one of the only people in the world who understood him. How was I supposed to focus on writing this paper when all I could think about was Roman?

Then it all clicked. Missing mothers were all the rage in fairy tales. I wanted to write about something new. I decided to focus my attention on the one character in the Angela Carter book that I could completely relate to—Wolf-Alice.

thirteen

Regardless of Kevin's assurance that Roman was in good hands, we all soon discovered that the unthinkable had occurred.

"Guys, we have something serious to discuss," said Kevin when I asked him how Roman was doing.

"This isn't the first complaint we've had about Roman. Over the years, he's had a few—not tons, but enough to red-flag him. He's been on probation with our organization, and I'm afraid this last complaint has put us in a very precarious position."

"Cut to the chase, man!" said Randy. "Where is he?"

Kevin continued. "We can't have a dog with that many strikes against him. We just can't."

"Where is he, Kevin?" I said. "We need to know the truth!"

Kevin was silent. Whatever he was about to tell us was grave. "He's at the pound."

I felt as though someone had punched me in the stomach and knocked the wind out of me.

"How could you let this happen?" Oak asked.

Kevin explained the bureaucracy of the system over and over again, as if the practicality of the rules and regulations was supposed to override the emotions of seeing Roman taken away without so much as a good-bye. I thought Kevin was supposed to be not only my advocate, but also the dogs'. He had let me down.

"It's not his fault," said Talbot, defending Kevin. But I didn't agree with her.

I tried to think realistically. "What can we do?" I wasn't going to let my anger distract me from trying to remedy the situation.

"I've been up all night trying to think of creative solutions. I just can't wrap my head around this one, guys. I'm so sorry," said Kevin with sadness in his voice.

✻

After class I urged the others to stay behind and discuss Roman's situation. We were a hodgepodge of delinquent talent, for sure—but what we all had in common was our ability to rebel and think outside the box. This had to work in our favor, if we could channel it correctly.

"We have to see him," I told the group.

"I have a date, Iris," said Randy.

"And I have to babysit my cousin. Sorry," said Shelley.

"I get it. It's fine," I said. "What about you two?" I asked Oak and Talbot. I knew they didn't completely get along with one another and Oak and I were still on the outs, but I'd hoped they could put aside their differences for Roman's sake.

"I'm in," said Talbot.

"Yeah, me too," said Oak.

The three of us piled into Oak's truck and headed toward the pound. Operation Dog Rescue was in full effect.

✻

"He's got to be in here somewhere," Oak said.

Oak, Talbot, and I were at the animal shelter, peering into all of the kennels, looking for Roman. I couldn't help but think how being stuck in a shelter was quite possibly the worst thing for a dog who was working so hard to overcome his past. Who would be brave enough to pick him as their ideal pet when the place was filled with younger, sweeter-looking dogs with all four legs intact?

The smell of the building, a strange mix of urine and bleach, each alternately overpowering the other, was reason enough to hate this place.

"What if they've adopted him out already?" asked Talbot.

"That should be the least of your concerns," said Oak.

"I forgot," she said, "you know everything."

I couldn't take their bickering. And the nonstop barking was enough to give anyone, human or animal, an anxiety attack.

"Can we remember for one second that this is about Roman and not about you two?" I couldn't believe they were getting into it at a time like this.

"Here he is!" shouted Talbot. Oak and I ran quickly to catch up to her.

Roman was in the very last enclosure, huddled in the corner, but he rose quickly and wagged his tail as soon as he heard our voices.

A big sign with the word AGGRESSIVE in block letters was hanging outside his cell. He had been labeled, like me. I thought about how even my own best friend had grown fearful of that label.

I reached my hands through the bars of his cell to pet him.

"Hiya, boy!"

He licked the salt off of my skin.

A husky, uniformed guard came running over to us. "Miss, I'm going to have to ask that you refrain from placing your hands in the cell. You never know with a dog like this. They can snap."

"Oh, they're old friends," said Talbot.

"Then maybe you'd like to consider adopting him? Once dogs are brought in, they don't have long before—well, you know," said the guard.

"Before what, exactly?" asked Oak.

"Before he's euthanized. Put down," he added, as if we didn't know what *euthanized* meant. "It's shelter policy. He's lucky he ended up here. The one over in Capitola has a standing order of just three days for unclaimed dogs."

"Well, how many days does he have left?" I asked, but the guard just shrugged.

My heart sank. In a matter of days, Roman, my rescue, would be killed, and there was nothing I could do about it.

"Can you take him home?" asked Oak.

"There's no way," I said. "We can't have animals at our place."

"My mom's really allergic," he said. "She can't get anywhere near dogs. She'd never be able to come in my room."

"Maybe that's not such a bad thing," said Talbot.

"Sorry," said Oak.

We both turned to Talbot.

"Don't look at me. You know I'd take all of them if I could. But I have an orange RV with my name on it that I'll be driving across this country in three hundred and sixty-five days, and bringing a dog with me on the road isn't part of the vision."

I was getting angry. Not at the fact that neither my friend nor my quasi-boyfriend would adopt Roman, but infuriated by how helpless the situation was.

"Is there any way we can hang out with him?" I asked the guard.

"Sure, you can have ten minutes in the visiting room. It's really only supposed to be for people who are considering adopting an animal. But you all seem like a nice bunch."

"We're not *that* nice," joked Talbot under her breath. I shot her a look, not wanting to jeopardize any time with my dog.

The guard brought a leash over to Roman, who retreated, shaking back into his corner when the cell was unlocked.

It was awful to see him like this. It made me think about how environment really was everything. How was an animal supposed to survive in a cage? I thought about the one day I had spent in jail and imagined what it would be like to be stuck there for days on end. What if no one had come to pick me up? What kind of life was it when there was no one to bail you out?

❀

"He's scared," I said. I could practically read Roman's thoughts at this point.

When the guard started heading toward Roman's neck to hook the leash, Roman barked viciously, making the guard jump.

"I don't think it's gonna happen today. Not worth getting my arm bitten off," the guard said to me.

"May I try?" I asked.

"She's really good with him," said Oak.

"It's against policy," said the guard.

"Sometimes, policies suck," said Talbot.

Before the guard could respond, Roman was at my feet, begging.

"See?" said Talbot.

"All right, but don't tell them up front." The guard handed me the leash, and I easily clipped it to Roman's collar.

"Walks well on a leash. I never would have guessed that," said the confounded guard as he escorted us to the end of the hall, then led us to a room with a few beaten-up dog toys.

"I trained him," I said proudly.

"You have ten minutes," the guard said and left us alone.

Once the guard shut the door, Roman's personality came out. He wasn't scared or defensive but loving and playful, tugging on a rope and digging at a plastic tube filled with dog treats.

"He doesn't belong here," said Talbot.

"We need to find Sebastian's dad. It's the only way," I said.

"Who's Sebastian?" asked Oak.

"The kid, from the park," I said. "The one with the kite. If he could learn about who Roman really is, how much he means to all of us…"

"It's never gonna work. That guy hates dogs. He really believed that Roman was going to attack his kid," said Talbot.

I couldn't take my gaze off of Roman.

"Well, it's the only choice we have," I said.

After Roman had tired himself out running around he nuzzled in close to me, leaning his face up against my knee as I stroked his head. He breathed a few deep breaths, like a dog who had the whole weight of the world on his shoulders.

"You're gonna be okay," I whispered, not believing my own words. But maybe, if he heard them, he'd sleep better tonight.

And then, as if life was racing by at warp speed, the guard was at the door telling us our time was up.

"I'll let you put the leash back on," he said.

I obliged and led Roman back to his cell.

"We love you, Roman," said Talbot.

"We miss you," added Oak.

I lowered my face down to Roman's, and for the first time I saw that we were two similar beings, struggling to contain our anger. Struggling to be understood.

"We'll get you out of here," I said, handing the leash over to the guard, who opened the door and made sure Roman was locked back inside.

✿

We spent all of Saturday hanging out at the grassy knoll at Natural Bridges, desperately waiting for Sebastian and his dad to show up. Even Shelley and Randy joined us.

"I can't say I even like that dog, but I like you," Randy said to me; my cheeks reddened.

It was all to no avail. Tons of kids passed through with Frisbees, their own dogs, jump ropes, and picnics. But no sign of the boy.

The clock was ticking.

"Let's follow the ice cream cart," said Shelley.

"I'm not worried about eating ice cream right now," said Talbot, annoyed.

"Not to eat, you fool," she said. "The ice cream cart is like the Pied Piper for little kids!"

She had a point—everywhere that cart went with its ringing bell, kids came running. Unfortunately, just not the kid we were looking for.

"What are we going to do?" Talbot asked.

My brain was racing with ideas. I had always been a good student, able to critically think. Why, then, was I completely frozen when it came to this dog rescue?

"We could talk to Kevin?" suggested Talbot.

"Again?" I said. "We've bugged him about this like ten times. He won't budge. He thinks that dad has a right to his opinions as much as we have a right to ours."

"He doesn't want to jeopardize his organization," said Oak.

"Maybe we could break into the pound and get Roman out?" said Talbot.

"No way I'd risk it. One more infraction for me, and I'm gonna get real jail time instead of this community service stuff," said Randy.

"Randy's right. We can't break the law again. It would be the ultimate irony," I said.

"You and your big words," said Shelley.

We were exhausted, sunburned, and stressed out. Everyone wanted to go home, but no one wanted to be the first to admit it.

Finally, Shelley said, "I have another babysitting gig tonight," prompting all of us to stand up and gather our things. I thought about Conor and Hunter, the boys I was supposed to have been sitting over the summer. I wondered who their new sitter was and if they liked her more than me.

"I have another hot date," said Randy.

"I have an obligatory family dinner. Anyone jealous?" said Talbot, rolling her eyes.

I was, but I didn't say anything.

"You two? Any plans?" asked Talbot.

"We do, actually. Big plans," said Oak.

I looked at him. We hadn't talked about having plans tonight. In fact, unless the conversation had been about Roman, we hadn't really talked at all since the bonfire.

Once everyone else had left, I didn't want it to be awkward to be alone with Oak, but it was. I tried to diffuse the situation by talking about Roman again.

"There's gotta be something more we can do," I said.

Oak was looking deeply into my eyes. "You're such a good person, Iris."

I blushed. It was good being this close to him. And just when I was about to return the compliment, he leaned in to kiss me. His lips were soft.

I pulled back. "Have you noticed we only kiss when the sun is setting?"

"What can I say?" said Oak. "I'm picky about mood lighting."

"Or maybe we're vampires," I offered.

He bared his teeth and then went in for another kiss.

"So you still like me?" I asked sheepishly.

"Yeah, you can't scare me away that easily," he said.

"I'm sorry about how I reacted before," I said, hoping Oak would understand me. "It's this thing I do. I'm not good at accepting help."

"I know. I get it. But remember, taking some help isn't the same as being rescued."

I nodded, and we kissed some more. And just as I was about to get lost in the moment, an idea came to me.

"We have to go," I said.

"What just happened? What did I do?"

"Nothing, it's not you. It's just…I think I've figured out a way to save Roman's life!"

"But we've exhausted every possibility," said Oak, frustrated.

"You're forgetting one small detail," I said. "You're a computer bad-boy genius!"

"What does that have to do with—"

"Can we go to your house?" I asked. "I have an idea."

✿

By the time we arrived at Oak's house, the fog had come creeping in, and we could barely see three feet in front of us. I removed my bike from the back of his truck, and, for the first time, I got to see his house, which was on the south side of town, near the beach, across from the Santa Cruz Beach Boardwalk—not very far from me.

"Hot beverage?" he offered.

"Have any coffee?" I asked.

"I have something better."

"What could be better than coffee?" I asked. It wouldn't hurt to skip the coffee so late in the day.

"Green tea."

I made a face, but minutes later, I took the cup of hot tea. It smelled like twigs.

"Not bad, right?" Oak said, watching me sip the tea.

"I guess," I said, unsure whether I enjoyed the nuttiness of the tea.

"You're drinking something over four thousand years old!" Oak said. The history buff was coming out. "You know, there's a legend that this guy was out walking in the countryside, boiling a pot of water under a tea tree, and some leaves fell into the pot. He tasted it and loved it and could sense it had medicinal properties and just like that, we got green tea!"

I could only finish some of it.

"Maybe it will grow on you?" Oak said, placing the half-empty mug in the sink.

I tried to stay in the moment, but my thoughts kept returning to Roman.

"So, we'll need your computer," I said, trying to get us back on track.

"Okay, it's in my room. Follow me."

I walked with Oak into his bedroom, which was a converted garage. There was lots of original artwork, posters of CD covers, and robotic-looking computer pieces arranged artistically across his wall.

On another wall was a big world map covered with pushpins with yellow heads at various locations, perhaps of places he wanted to go or places he had been.

Oak removed his sweatshirt, his body warmed from the tea. It was the first time he'd taken it off in front of me, and I tried to hide my curiosity in seeing a full view of his neck for the first time. I laughed to myself about how silly it was that I was getting so excited over a neck. But when he shifted in the other direction to turn on his computer, he revealed a large, jagged scar on the right side of his neck.

"What happened?" I asked involuntarily.

Oak realized his reveal and immediately reached up to the scar, covering it with his palm. It was as though he had forgotten it existed until I reminded him.

"Oh, fishing accident. I was ten. The hook was supposed to be cast out to the ocean, but I was a spastic ten-year-old and I was running all over that boat. It got me instead of some fish. There was a lot of blood."

I slowly walked over to Oak with my fingers reached out toward the raised scar on his neck. I thought about how much people have to go through in their lives. Dying parents. Bloody accidents. At times it felt like it was all too much.

But here Oak was, in front of me. Fine. Recovered. The scar his only evidence of the accident. Up close, it looked like a magnified section of a snowflake—the flesh of the scar a prominent pink protruding against his olive skin.

"It's beautiful," I said as I ran my finger down the scar.

"Well, no one's ever said that before."

"That's because no one's ever seen it before. You're always hiding it."

"I just don't want to answer all the questions," he said.

"I know what you mean."

We sat in silence for a moment, listening to the whir of his computers. "Hey, computer genius," I said.

"Yeah?"

"So here's my idea. It's pretty vague at this point, but I don't want to risk you having to get into trouble."

"For you, I'm all in," said Oak.

"So, there must be some way to hack into the pound's computer system, right?"

"I might be able to do it. But even if I could, then what? Transferring funds is way easier than transferring a dog in cyberspace."

"That's it!" I yelled.

"What?" he asked.

"What you said about funds. You can change numbers, right?"

"Yeah, I'm pretty good at that."

"Go to the pound website."

His fingers clacked across the keyboard, its letters faded from so much frantic typing. The site popped up on the screen in a matter of seconds.

"Bingo," Oak said. "Now what?"

"Find Roman."

Oak clicked through the pages of dogs listed, each with a photo of the dog, a short description of its estimated age plus its breed—and then, in red lettering, the days until the dog was to be euthanized. It was heartbreaking to see the staggering number of dogs waiting on the chopping block, with no way they could all be saved in time. What a life to live, suffering through neglect or abuse only to end up in a place like the pound, where you're given a warm meal and attention and, just when you think things are getting good again, your life is ended.

"Got him!" shouted Oak.

Up on the screen was Roman, looking courageous, the pain seeping through his eyes. Underneath his photo, the unlucky number one showed how many days he had left to live.

"Shepherd mix." Oak read his breed description. "Are they kidding?"

"It's what they call all pit bulls. No one wants to adopt them because of their bad reputation. And no mention of his missing leg! Guess they want someone to fall in love with him on the website and then show up and not care that he only has three legs."

"Like you did," said Oak.

"Exactly." I thought back to the first time Roman and I met and how much I was turned off by his appearance and the way he just seemed so angry. Not at all the way I thought of him now that I understood him.

"You sure you're up for this?" I asked.

"I'm not sure what I can do," Oak said. "I mean, I want to help. You know I'd do anything for Roman."

"Right, for Roman." I had to remind myself that of course it was all for the dog.

"And for you," he added.

I felt my cheeks warm. This was no time for romantic interludes. I had to snap out of it. "I need you to work your magic."

"What magic is that?" he asked.

"Oak, the computer-hacking wonder of the northern hemisphere—I need you to hack into that site and switch the days Roman has left to live."

A huge grin spread across his face.

"I think you're the one who's the computer genius," he said. "But there are a few kinks in your plan."

I felt short of breath all over again. If this didn't work, Roman would be killed tomorrow.

"This is the site for viewers, like us, interested in looking for a dog," he said.

I wasn't following.

"The employees probably don't even look at this page. We need to hack deeper..."

"Get to the interior calendar and files." I was finally catching on.

"Exactly!" Oak said.

Before we could celebrate our plan, Oak's fingers were once again racing across the keys like a professional pianist's. The screen went black, and what looked like gibberish started scrolling across it in white lettering.

"What's that?"

"Code...it's giving me its language. I have to figure out how to communicate with the system in order to infiltrate."

I watched as letters and symbols flew across the screen at record speed. Oak was hardly blinking. This computer code was a completely new language to me, but Oak was fluent. Then the stream of letters and numbers stopped.

"What happened?"

"It wants a password."

"Let's start guessing. What would a pound use as a password? Lassie, Benji..." I rattled off more names of famous dogs that I thought for sure a pound would use.

"Hunt-and-peck isn't going to work. I have a formula. I used it to break passwords all the time; it's how I hacked into those people's credit card accounts. We don't get to see their actual password, but it creates a temporary one that should let us in."

The typing continued until the screen paused a second time.

"It froze," I said.

"It's thinking," said Oak. "And we're in!" He smacked his hand down on the desk. On the screen we could see the inner workings of the pound, from security cameras to each dog's file. Oak navigated his way to Roman's profile page.

"There it is, day to be euthanized—August fourteenth."

I watched as the cursor moved backwards over the anticipated date and...

"It disappeared!" I said.

"Like magic." Oak began typing again. "August seventeenth."

"That only gives us three extra days!"

"I can't make it too obvious. You heard the guard; dogs don't last long in those places. If I make it two weeks from today, they'll know something is up. I mean, I can, if that's what you want."

I thought it over. "No, you're right. I don't want to run the risk of you getting in trouble again." While I felt heaps better about Roman's situation, I knew it was only a temporary relief because the problem had not been resolved, just prolonged.

"Then that's it. We just bought him three more days of life." And with one last click of a button, Oak exited the screen, and his desktop returned to its photo of Oak and his dad camping in the Redwoods.

"Thank you," I said, grateful for Oak's willingness to help.

"Don't thank me yet. Roman isn't out of trouble. Far from it."

"No, thank you...for trying. For taking a chance on him. On me," I stuttered. Speaking my true feelings embarrassed me, but the words had been said honestly, and that was the best I could do.

Oak was leaning toward me, and I moved to reach him. When our lips touched I felt it everywhere, like fireworks were exploding all over my body. It had never been this way with Andy. We never had that sort of connection.

"Iris Moody, will you be my girlfriend?"

And, just like that, Roman had acquired three more days of life, and I had acquired a boyfriend.

✿

After a make-out session that left my lips sore, we were lying on Oak's bed, staring up at the glow-in-the-dark constellation stickers on his ceiling.

"Those guys are nice," I said, talking about our Ruff Rehabilitation team.

"Yeah, they are. The only one I—" he stopped himself midsentence.

"What?" I asked.

"It's nothing," he said. "Sometimes I should learn to keep my big mouth shut."

"Okay, now you *have* to tell me what you were going to say."

"The only one who kind of rubs me the wrong way is Talbot."

I had seen them bicker before, so I shouldn't have been too shocked, but I just assumed it wasn't so severe, since he knew she and I were becoming such good friends.

"Well, what don't you like about her?" I asked, wanting to understand his position.

He thought for a moment. "I guess just the whole scandal thing."

This set me off. Here was a girl who clearly had been taken advantage of, and Oak was vilifying the victim. I thought about what Perry had said in English class regarding how women in fairy tales were represented either as princesses or witches. Perry called this "polarization," and here was Oak, who seemed to be doing the exact same thing. *The waters rose speedily* as I grew defensive; Oak had

176

become the voice of patriarchy that always blamed women.

I sat up. "What her teacher did—I mean, he was the adult, Oak. She's the kid. She was really in love with him, and it takes two to tango. Why would he be in jail right now if what he did wasn't wrong?"

"Whoa, calm down," he said, sitting up.

"Don't tell me to calm down." I jumped off his bed. Whatever closeness I had felt toward him minutes before disappeared.

"She's the only one you've heard about this from, right?" he asked.

I nodded. "So? What's your point?"

"So did you ever think that maybe there might be more to this than what you've been told?"

"What does this have to do with anything?" I asked.

"What was the name of the guy, the teacher?"

"Mr. Ettinger," I said. Talbot still talked about him so much—how could I forget? I remembered our conversation in her room, where I'd listened intently as she told me the whole story.

Oak was back at his computer and within seconds was clicking on the "faculty" tab on the Clark Academy website. Teachers' profile photos filled the screen. Oak typed Mr. Ettinger's name into the search window. Up popped the same photograph Talbot had shown me, framed and hidden in her room.

"Yeah, that's him. So what?"

"So what? You're not connecting the dots here. According to Talbot, they were caught hooking up and now he's in jail for making advances on a minor, correct?"

"That's right."

"Well, if he's in jail, how come he's currently on faculty at Clark?"

I pondered this for a moment. "Maybe the site hasn't been updated?"

"You really think a school would be so negligent as to leave a convicted sex offender listed as current faculty?" asked Oak.

He had a point.

"I need more proof," I said. I was a woman of science. What Oak had was merely a hypothesis. One piece of evidence did not a theory make.

He clicked on Mr. Ettinger's photo. A list of high school science classes came up, including one he supposedly was teaching this summer. Oak clicked on the link, which led to a page that included a summary of everything they had covered on Friday, including a homework assignment.

Mr. Ettinger wasn't in jail. He was in Santa Cruz teaching summer school.

I sat back down on Oak's bed. "I don't get it."

"My buddy Ry goes to Clark. He told me a whole different story. In ninth grade Talbot became obsessed with a boy named Ben Platt. She called him all the time and got herself transferred into his classes. She joined the cheerleading squad to be close to him because he played football. She was stalking him, Iris. It got so bad that Ben's parents pulled him out of the school. He goes to Harbor now. She did the same thing with Mr. Ettinger. She wouldn't leave him alone. She told everyone they were dating, but it just wasn't true. She tried to make a move on him, and he called campus security and then the administration intervened."

"But her parents had a restraining order put on him," I said, still trying to process everything Oak had just told me.

"It's the other way around. She flipped out when she found out he had a fiancée. He's got a restraining order on *her*."

I couldn't believe that my new friend had lied to me. I felt completely betrayed.

"I'm sorry to be the one to break it to you, but you should know the truth. I just want you to know what kind of person you're dealing with."

Like the fairy tales that morphed with each retelling, Talbot's story had shifted. It seemed like everything around me was changing its trajectory, from Talbot's story about Mr. Ettinger to Roman's plight to my declining relationship with my dad.

I wanted everyone and everything to freeze, just for a while, so I could find my bearings. The only absolute truth I could conclude was there was no such thing as an absolute truth.

fourteen

Aside from texting everyone to let them know that Roman had been spared for three more days, I avoided Talbot's calls and texts all weekend until I could figure out how to deal with the situation.

I could barely concentrate in Perry's class on Monday morning. Between the butterflies in my stomach as I replayed kissing Oak and his official declaration of the two of us being together to my nervousness that with each passing second, the likelihood of finding Kite Boy and his dad were dwindling, I was totally unprepared for Perry's pop quiz on Vladimir Propp's formalist approach to a narrative structure. I thought it had been a shorter reading assignment that I could cram in that morning, but it was way long. The content just wasn't sticking.

I wasn't the only one who was having an off day. Two guys in class, Todd and José, had been mouthing off the entire morning, even after Perry asked them to stop and then made them switch seats so they weren't near each other. I could tell she was at her wit's end when she finally lost her temper (it was the first time I'd seen that except for when she had defended me that first day) and made us read an essay on archetypes in our reader for the rest of the period while she graded our quizzes.

Reading was the last thing I could focus on. Every time I came to the end of a sentence, I'd forget what I had just read about and have to start all over. There was just too much on my mind. Finally, after thirty minutes of staring at words that didn't stick, the bell rang and everyone gathered their things.

Perry rose from her desk. "Iris, a word with you, please."

This wasn't going to be pretty. I knew I had done terribly on that quiz, but I thought I'd at least bought myself until the next class to be confronted about it.

"What's going on?" Perry asked once everyone had cleared the room.

"I'm sorry about that," I said, looking down at the quiz, full of purple ink marks (Perry thought that red ink was the stigma of smarmy old-school teachers).

"You can do so much better than this," Perry said. "So tell me what's going on."

I was disappointed in myself. "The truth?" I asked.

Perry nodded. "Always, please."

"I forgot about the homework."

"That much is clear. The question I'm asking is why?"

My instinct was to lie—make up a story about my dad or my bike or say that our house had been robbed and they stole the book, or I had been taking the book everywhere with me and I left it at the market and they finally found it this morning and they were holding it for me. But the last thing Perry was asking for was a fabrication.

So I decided to go with the truth. "The dog, the one I've been working with at my community service—they took him away from me. They think he's too aggressive, but he's really not. It's all just because he's a pit bull and now he's at the pound and he's going to be killed tomorrow and I can't stop it!" I couldn't hold back the tears.

"I'm so sorry, Iris." She leaned in to hug me.

I continued. "And there's this guy and he's so great and I think he really likes me and he has me so distracted I can't think about anything else but him."

"You should have just stuck with the first excuse," said Perry.

I laughed. "I wanted to tell you the whole truth."

"I know. And I appreciate it. It sounds like you have a lot going on," she said.

I nodded.

"But you need to find a way to make school a priority. There's a lot riding on this class for you. It can open doors for you or close them. You're an excellent English student. A great critical thinker. I don't want this to be a class strictly about English but also about how to 'read' people's situations. If you can learn to navigate and negotiate pages in a text—you're set for life! You are doing so well! You don't want to throw away all your hard work by 'forgetting' about assignments all of a sudden. You need to make this class more important—which means making yourself more important."

"I know. I will. I promise." And I meant it.

"Can I show you something?" she asked.

She leaned down and retrieved her green canvas army bag, pulling out her wallet.

"I want to show you Dante, my baby," Perry said.

I didn't realize she had kids. She handed me a photo. It was a dog. I smiled.

Finding a fellow dog lover had become a secret code of acknowledgment, like we all instantly understood the love capable between human and dog.

"He's so cute! How old is he?" I asked.

Her face washed over with sadness.

"It's hard for me to talk about him in the past tense. He died last year. I had some friends staying with me. They left the gate open. Dante ran out in the street just as a car was coming." She stopped talking. I could tell that it was still a difficult subject to broach.

"Chihuahua mix?" I asked.

"You got it! At the pound, they said the mom was a lab and the dad was a Chihuahua. I don't buy it. Could you imagine the logistics?"

I blushed and then handed the photo back to Perry.

"He used to bring me the paper every morning. He had such a little mouth, yet he could still carry that bulky newspaper over to me."

Then I got an idea.

"I know it might be too soon, but all the dogs we're rehabilitating are up for adoption!" I said, hopeful.

"Iris, I don't know. There will never be another dog like Dante."

I fantasized about the possibility of Perry adopting Roman, but I had an awful nagging feeling that in a few days he wouldn't even make it to graduation.

"You're probably right about that," I said, "but there could be a completely different but equally wonderful dog. There's my dog, Roman. He has three legs, but it doesn't slow him down."

"I'm more of a small dog kinda gal, Iris."

"We have a Chihuahua," I said. "Her name is Tinkerbelle. I'm sure you can change her name. She's totally trained, potty trained, everything."

Perry looked off into the distance. It was time for the icing on the cake.

"She even knows how to retrieve a paper," I said.

She looked back at me. "Really?"

"Yup. And she's amazingly good at it, too." I wrote down the name of the Ruff Rehabilitation website so she could check it out later.

"Thanks," she said, putting the paper in her purse.

"Thank you," I said, grabbing my failed assignment off her desk. "I promise I'll do better."

Perry nodded. "Don't make that promise to me. Make it to yourself."

As I left, I thought about how I'd actually managed to not think about Oak for the last ten minutes.

Then I thought about him the entire way to dog training.

☼

Kevin had a new dog, a peppy dalmatian mix on a leash, and handed the leash to me when I got there. "This is Sid."

I hated Sid immediately, but only because he was a constant reminder that Roman wasn't here. When it came down to it, Sid was a fine dog—young and sprightly and easy to train. Apparently, his owner was an alcoholic and regularly forgot to feed him. But he'd made a lot of progress and, as Kevin put it, wasn't as "damaged" as some of the others. He'd be easy to adopt out, with his floppy ears and bouncy gait.

Oak patted Sid on the head when he came over to hug me. His sweatshirt was off. I smiled.

"Something about him is different," said Talbot when he left to practice heeling with his dog.

"No hood," I said.

"Oh, wow!" said Talbot. "What a difference a hood makes!"

I still wasn't sure how I wanted to handle the situation now that I knew the truth about her. I just knew I could no longer trust her.

Everyone else was instructed to go through the entire repertoire with their dogs except for me. Since Sid was new to the program, he needed to catch up, so I was back to *sit* and *stay*. And, just as I finally got him to stay for the first time, his concentration was broken by Talbot, who was all the way across the grass, screaming her head off about something. I tried to ignore her dramatics.

"Bite toy!" I thought I heard her shout, and I wondered when that sort of command would come in handy. Everyone was looking toward her, and when Sid and I moved closer to see what was going on, I deciphered what Talbot been screaming.

"Kite Boy!" It finally came out clearly.

I ran over to the group and saw the boy, Sebastian, with a new kite, and his father, now at the opposite end of the park—as far away from our dogs as possible.

Without thinking I handed Sid's leash over to Kevin and bolted in that direction. Everyone else did the same, and Kevin was left with all five dogs while we ran full speed toward the boy, who had just gotten his kite airborne.

When Sebastian's dad recognized us, he started frantically reeling in the kite, apparently thinking we were out for vengeance.

"Wait!" I shouted as the father took his son by the hand and started heading toward the parking lot. "We want to talk to you!"

"If this is about the dog, I don't want to talk about it."

"Listen, you jerk!" said Talbot.

I shot her a look that said, "Shut up!" and approached the boy's dad.

"Sir, I understand why Roman spooked you." I spoke clearly, with confidence, so he'd take me seriously.

"Thank you," he said, sincerely appreciative of the acknowledgment.

"I was scared, too, the first time I met him," I admitted.

"And the second time!" added Oak.

"And the third," said Randy.

"It's true," I said. "I was totally afraid that he was going to rip my face off. That's what I thought pit bulls did. But not Roman. He was abused for over seven years. They raised him to be a killer fighting dog, and he was a champion. They also left him tied to a chain for weeks on end and didn't feed him or even give him water, and they left him in the blistering sun. What kind of caregiver does that?"

We both looked over to the boy, who was trying to get a knot out of the kite string.

I continued, "He wasn't after your kid. He saw the awkward movement of the kite. When it hovered and then swooped down suddenly—he thought he was being attacked."

The dad looked sympathetic. "Look, I'm sorry about what happened. But I'm a dad and my number one priority is Sebastian, not your dog. He shouldn't have run over to us. It's probably better for him to be contained somewhere, in someone's yard, where he can't go around scaring people like that."

"Oh, he's contained all right," said Talbot.

"They're putting him to sleep tomorrow," I said.

The boy approached us with his tangled kite in hand. "Daddy, what does that mean?" he asked, looking up at his father with his big brown eyes. I hadn't even realized he had been listening.

"It means they're going to kill him!" said Talbot, unable to control herself. I let her speak. She was telling the truth. The kid had a right to know, however harsh it sounded.

"Daddy! You can't let them kill the dog!" Tears streamed down the boy's face.

I wanted to scoop the boy up and hug him for his innocent empathy.

The dad looked at his son. "What happens to that dog is *not* my concern," he said.

Sebastian was now crying, not even letting his father console him. His dad sighed a deep sigh. "What can I do?"

I explained the plan. "You can go to the pound today, right now, and revise the statement you made that got him into that place. Talk them into releasing him back to Ruff Rehabilitation. You're a lawyer. You must be able to produce a convincing argument."

I had him there. Either he was a good enough lawyer to convince them, or he would fail and prove himself a bad lawyer. His pride was at stake.

"Will you save the dog, Daddy?" asked Sebastian.

The father looked at his son, then at us. "Like I said, I'd do anything for my kid."

We all erupted in hugs and smiles, and when I finally came up for air from a big, seven-person bear hug, I noticed Kevin, flanked by our dogs, beaming proudly.

❁

According to Kevin, it didn't take long for Sebastian's dad to write down his retraction and clear it with Ruff Rehabilitation. Kevin then buzzed down to the pound to release Roman. We didn't tell Kevin about how Oak hacked into the system, thereby actually saving Roman from certain death. We were pretty sure that despite our best intentions, he wouldn't have approved of Oak breaking the law.

I'd still have to wait until the following Monday to be reunited with Roman. Kevin wanted to keep an eye on him before bringing him back to the group. I tried plunging myself into schoolwork. Oak was away on a camping trip, which was probably a good thing, so I could try to focus all of my attention on my final paper for Perry's class.

She had loved it when I had shared with her my idea for my final paper: "Little Red Goes Rogue: Wolf-Alice Redefines the Female Hero in Fairy Tales." My argument would be that "Little Red Riding Hood" works to victimize the female character. She is punished for trying to choose her own destiny. She is misled, manipulated, eaten, and then rescued, whereas Wolf-Alice begins as a misunderstood and wild creature who cannot be tamed by others. Instead she changes from within once she learns about compassion. Wolf-Alice is responsible for her own journey, mistakes and all. This was definitely a topic that I could personally relate to.

fifteen

It was amazing how much easier it was to concentrate on English when there were no distractions. Things were good with Oak, Roman was safe, and I tried my best to stop myself from thinking about Talbot's lying. And, just like with Ashley and Sierra, I was back to avoiding Talbot's texts and phone calls. I knew I had to confront her, but I didn't know how to bring it up.

Even better, the cable had been inexplicably turned on, and the delinquent notices ceased to gather in our mailbox. I was ecstatic that Dad had actually followed through on something. And somehow, with all the work I had on my hands, I exhibited enough self-control to limit my TV viewing to an hour a day. With all the experience I'd gained over the summer with the dogs, I felt as though I could be hosting my own show on the animal network.

I had been working for two hours straight and had about a five-page rough draft. Everyone in "Wolf-Alice" seemed so shocked when she learned compassion all on her own, not just because someone else told her to be that way. I immediately thought about Roman and the first few days when he'd ignored my commands. He didn't trust me then. Why should he have listened to me? What authority did I have?

I was just hitting my stride when the phone rang. I shouldn't have answered it, but my instincts got the best of me.

"Emergency field trip. Right now," said Talbot.

"What are you talking about?"

"I just discovered the cutest pet store ever down on Pacific. Meet me here in ten." She hung up before I could say anything.

Maybe it was a good idea to take a break. Besides, Perry had recently told us that in order to complete mental tasks, it was imperative that we take breaks. And I really wanted to get something special to give to Roman for his graduation.

As I strapped on my bike helmet, I got a text from Talbot. *Meet me at Pergolesi. Dying for something iced.*

Fifteen minutes later, I was locking my bike to a parking meter down the street from the coffee shop. I took off my backpack and removed a stack of papers.

"Hi! What's that?" Talbot asked, referring to the paperwork now cradled in my arms.

I had been doing some thinking, and since I wasn't going to be hired for any babysitting gigs anytime soon, I'd decided to print up some flyers advertising my services as a basic dog trainer. The flyers were nothing fancy—just a photo of a golden retriever I found online, along with the words IRIS MOODY: DOG TRAINER and my home phone number. I'd also printed some extra flyers that Kevin had given us announcing our Ruff Rehabilitation graduation ceremony.

Talbot helped me staple them to telephone poles and trees as we walked toward the coffee shop.

Pergolesi was packed with people on the porch enjoying the afternoon sun. I had a feeling of rushed excitement, which I got whenever summer was coming to an end—this need to cram everything in. And, with what limited time I had each day, I also felt this driving desire to make up for lost time.

As luck would have it, Ashley was working. It's not that things were bad between us now. They were tolerable. But that's what made me feel so awful about the whole situation. I didn't want our relationship to pass muster. I wanted it to be comfortable.

As we got closer and closer to the front of the line, I wondered how she would react to seeing me today. Friend or foe?

"Hey, Eye!" said Ashley, when I reached the front. I was relieved she was receiving me with kindness.

"Hi," said Talbot.

"Oh, sorry. Ashley, this is Talbot. She's doing that dog rehab thing with me." It was weird introducing the two of them—my two different worlds colliding at the coffee shop.

"Iced coffee, Eye?" Ashley asked, knowing this was my favorite mid-afternoon drink on a hot day.

"Can I make it an iced green tea?" I asked.

"Really?" She was surprised.

"It's a new thing I'm trying," I said, not wanting to go into all the details about Oak.

"Not me. I'll have the biggest iced coffee you have. With extra whipped cream!" Talbot licked her lips like a kid about to devour a banana split.

As Ashley gave us our drinks, Talbot handed her one of our graduation flyers.

"What's this?" asked Ashley.

"It's what we've been working on all summer," I said. "With the dogs. They're showing off all their tricks," I explained.

"And getting new homes," interjected Talbot.

"You hate dogs!" said Ashley.

"I *hated* dogs," I said. "People can change."

As Talbot and I left the bustling coffee house, I hoped that Ashley thought I had changed into the kind of person she wanted to hang out with again.

We walked to Talbot's discovery, The Golden Leash, an upscale pet boutique on Pacific.

"What are you thinking of getting him?" asked Talbot.

"I don't know."

I looked around at everything they had to offer: leashes in every color, argyle sweaters, ice cream for dogs. People sure spent a lot of money on their pets.

"What about this?" Talbot held up a bejeweled pooper-scooper.

"No way," I said.

"I think I'm gonna get this for Garrett," said Talbot, holding up a bottle of bright pink, glittery doggy nail polish.

"You think Kevin will be cool with that?"

"Just for graduation. I mean, he has to look good for his new owners, right?"

I had been avoiding thinking about Roman's new owner. More than anything, I wanted him to be adopted out to a new family. But I was also deeply jealous that someone else would get to see him every day. No one could love that dog like I could. And what was more troubling was the possibility that no one would want to adopt him and he would be back in the same predicament—back to the pound, waiting to be killed. No amount of hacking could save him from an eventual death if he ended up back at that shelter.

We wouldn't be meeting the dogs' new families until graduation day. And in most cases, we wouldn't even know if they had been adopted out before the actual ceremony. A lot of scrambling was involved on behalf of Ruff Rehabilitation—they couldn't officially start looking for adoptive families until the dogs completed their training program (our last class), which was a week away, and then Kevin had between then and graduation, one week later, to secure homes for the dogs, which included a home visit and two meetings with the potential owners.

After scanning the shelves, I finally saw the perfect gift. Among the snazzy and over-the-top pet products was a perfectly understated orange collar. I liked that the box said it was made out of something called "pleather" and that no animals were used or harmed in the making of the product. But the best part was that etched on the inside of the collar, where no one else could see, were the words *I am loved.*

It would be my constant message to Roman, and it made the possibility of him being taken home by another family a little more bearable.

"How much is this?" I asked the woman at the counter.

"Twenty-five bucks," she said.

"For a collar?" I complained. It seemed awfully high.

Talbot came over to me. "We're at a high-end pet store. What did you expect? We can run to Petmart if you want?"

"They won't have that collar there, miss," said the cashier. "These are a special import from Germany."

I didn't care where it was made; I needed to have it. Roman had to have this collar.

"I'll take it," I said, pulling out my wallet and giving the woman my debit card.

She took it and ran it though her machine. After a beep, the woman handed the card back to me.

"This card has been declined. Do you have another?" she asked.

I showed her my wallet. Aside from a few crinkled-up receipts and my driver's license, which I never had real use for except as photo identification, the wallet was empty.

"I don't understand," I said, both to the woman and to Talbot.

"Maybe it's because you haven't used it in a while. You always use cash," said Talbot.

That was true. But the account had over $20,000 in it—all of the money my mom had left me. It seemed like a little twenty-five-dollar dog collar wouldn't be enough to confuse the bank that much.

"What would you like to do?" asked the cashier with an attitude; it was clear she was growing annoyed with us. "It's the last collar, you know."

"Nice sales tactic, lady," Talbot said to the woman, who raised her eyebrow at her in return. Talbot reached into her bag. "Look, Iris, I'll spot you the money."

"You don't have to do that," I said.

"Yes, I do. That's what friends are for. And then we'll go straight to your bank and figure this out." She handed the cashier the money and waited for change. I took the collar and put it in my backpack.

Grabbing one of my flyers, Talbot handed it to the cashier. "The least you could do is hang up one of these behind your counter."

The woman eyed the flyer before pinning it to the bulletin board behind her cash register.

Outside, the sun glared down on us. I had forgotten to put sunscreen on before my ride and knew I would regret it.

There was a long line at First Pacific Bank. Talbot filled out some informational card for me (that girl loved filling out forms), and I grabbed a cup of the free coffee. I knew it was a step back in my caffeine-weaning process, but the situation was stressing me out.

The coffee was overly roasted and too acidic; I didn't even enjoy it.

"That stuff has got to be gross," said Talbot.

"But it's free. And if you load it up with sugar, it masks how awful it is. Want some?"

Talbot leaned in to sniff it. "No thanks," she said.

"Wanna hear something gross?" I asked.

She nodded.

"These Styrofoam cups weigh less after you drink from them, which means your body is ingesting some of the Styrofoam."

"Shouldn't that be illegal?" asked Talbot.

We had a seat on a couch in the small seating area next to other people holding their little pieces of paper with their number on it.

A girl, maybe a year older than us, was signing up for a college bank account with her mom and dad—yet another scene that, in my life, would never be played out.

"Number forty-one!" a voice finally called over the loudspeaker.

"That's us!" said Talbot.

I filled my cup back to the top and proceeded to our assigned teller.

"Identification," said the man, who couldn't have looked more bored.

I gave him my license.

"Ms. Moody, what can I do for you today?" he asked.

It had been a while since I'd had coffee, and it hit my system at warp speed.

"I just tried to use my bank card at the pet store, and it was declined. It was only for twenty-five dollars, so I was wondering why."

"Can I please see it?" the man asked.

I handed him my card. He quickly typed digits into his computer.

"In order to be able to withdraw twenty-five dollars from your account, you have to have at least twenty-five dollars in the account, Ms. Moody," he said with a snarky grin.

"What?" I was dumbfounded.

"Your account is nearly empty, Ms. Moody," the teller said. "That's why your card was declined."

I wanted to sock him in the face. But before I could get enraged over his attitude I had to get to the bottom of why the computer was saying the account was empty.

"Are you sure you have the right account? I mean, I just got a statement from you like two weeks ago saying that there was over"— and I leaned in to whisper, not wanting everyone to hear my personal finances—"twenty thousand dollars in that account."

The teller leaned in and whispered back to me, "Perhaps you made a large purchase in the last two weeks that you are forgetting about."

That was it. This guy was officially a royal jerk, and I was running out of patience. Talbot stepped in to save me from clobbering him. I moved aside and tried to focus on a deep-breathing technique that Doug had given me.

"Jake," Talbot said, reading his nametag. "You look like a man who is well-versed in computers. Can you please look at Ms. Moody's account activities over the last two weeks and see if perhaps anything unusual happened between the time that statement was mailed to her until now?"

My hands were suddenly damp; in my rage, I had clenched my fingers around the coffee cup so tightly I'd punctured a hole in the Styrofoam. The keys on Jake's computer clacked away.

"Ah, here we go…perhaps it slipped your mind that you withdrew twenty thousand dollars last Thursday?" He swiveled the screen around so that I could see it. I squinted my eyes, analyzing the data in front of me. The account balance was $10.41.

"But I didn't do that. I've never even been in here before, except to open the account with my dad."

"How old are you, Ms. Moody?" asked Jake, who was now my mortal enemy.

"Sixteen. Surely you can do the simple math to figure that out, given the fact that my birth year is glaring you in the face." I motioned toward his computer screen. If I couldn't overtly pummel him, at least I could do it verbally.

Talbot took over. "Have you had any breaches in security recently?" she asked. It made me laugh. I thought about Oak and how he could probably have hacked into my account or anyone else's if he wanted to. But he'd never do something like that again. Not even for me.

As I buried my head in my hands, Talbot put her arms around me. I shimmied away, recoiling at her attempt to console me.

I had helped her overcome her fear of the ocean. I had to let her help me here. I thought about what Oak had said about how letting someone come to your aid wasn't the same as being rescued. I realized it was okay to have my friends help me out.

I felt desperate. "This just makes no sense! It's my bank account! My money! I never spent it."

"Did anyone else have access to the account?" asked Jake, still refusing to believe that I had nothing to do with this.

"It's my account. I mean, the only other person on the account is..."

The wheels in my head were spinning faster than I could catch up with them. My cosigner. The only other person who had access to this account until I turned eighteen was my dad.

The pieces of the puzzle came together, first in fragments and then in large chunks. It was Dad—the same guy who was always lecturing me about doing the right thing and making the right choice.

My own father had taken money from me.

My college endowment was gone.

Dad had stolen my future.

I left Talbot with the teller at the counter and ran out of the bank. Talbot was chasing after me.

"Hey! Slow down!" she yelled.

But I continued running.

"Iris! Stop!"

I listened.

"What happened in there?" asked Talbot when I sat down on the grimy curb in front of Streetlight, a used record store. "What's going on?"

"My dad. He's the one who took the money."

She seemed as shocked as I was that my dad had been capable of this. Both of us were stunned into silence.

"Maybe your mom could talk to him. She wouldn't let your dad do something like this."

The last thing I wanted to talk about was my mom.

"You don't know anything about my mom," I said rudely.

"No, I don't—because you never tell me anything. I haven't even met your parents. I never come over to your place. I'm kind of getting a complex, Iris. Am I that much of an embarrassment to you?"

I knew I'd been vague with her about my family situation, but she acted so nonchalant about it I didn't realize she had been taking it personally.

It was time to tell her the truth.

"You don't get it," I said. "There *is* no Mom," I finally confessed. I didn't care about hiding my secret any longer. I was too upset.

Talbot looked confused.

"She's dead," I clarified.

Talbot put her hand to her mouth. "Oh my God. Iris, I'm so sorry."

"Just don't," I said.

"I'm not trying to offend you."

"Well, you are," I said.

Talbot's expression turned from empathetic to suspicious. "I don't understand. Why would you lie about your mom being alive?"

Instead of dealing with her question head-on, I turned it around and made it about her.

"I don't know, Talbot. Why would you lie to me about Mr. Ettinger? He's not in jail. He's still at Clark, teaching summer school." I knew I should be focusing on the situation with my dad, but it seemed easier to shift the blame to Talbot since she was the one sitting next to me. I had become an attack dog, jumping at any chance to tear my friend apart.

"Who told you?" she asked quietly.

"It doesn't matter," I said. Then I asked, "Do you still love him?"

Talbot shook her head. "It was never really love, just infatuation. I thought if I talked about it enough I'd be able to control the situation. I tend to get fixated on guys. I never meant for my feelings toward Mr. E. to become so out of control. I'm just so embarrassed."

"We all make mistakes, Talbot," I said.

"I wanted it to be true so badly," she said. "I thought if I could write my own story, then maybe it would play out just the way I wanted it to, you know?"

"Yeah, I know. I guess it's the same reason I made up a story about my mom being alive. But just because you say it out loud doesn't mean it's true."

"You're so right," said Talbot.

We sat quietly for a while, both of us contemplating how messed up we'd become.

Talbot finally broke the silence. "What happened? If you want to tell me."

"Drunk driver." I didn't need to say any more. I could see on Talbot's face that she was thinking about how she could have ended someone's life when she drove drunk.

"I guess your dad really needed that money," said Talbot.

"It's no excuse," I said.

"I know. Are you gonna call him?" she asked.

"Yeah, I guess I'll have to," I said.

Talbot stayed with me as I called Dad on his cell phone. It went straight to voice mail, which informed me that his mailbox was full. I called his work number and dialed his extension. Another automated voice announced that I had pressed an invalid entry and I was being transferred to the operator. I told her I was looking for my dad.

"Mr. Moody doesn't work here anymore," she said.

I was shocked. "Since when?"

"I'd say it's been about three weeks," said the woman on the other end of the phone.

The lying had to stop. I would go home and wait for Dad to return.

"Just remember what you told me," Talbot shouted as I hopped on my bike.

"What's that?" I said.

"We all make mistakes," she said.

✻

I didn't know exactly what I would say to Dad when I got home.

But I could measure my anger by how fast I was pedaling up the San Lorenzo Boulevard hill—the same hill I usually had to get off my bike and walk up.

Because of my adrenaline-fueled bike ride, I got home much faster than usual. I didn't bother locking Dad's bike to the fence before running full speed past the neighbor's barking dog, straight to my closet. I tried turning the lights on, but the electricity was out. I flashed back to the shutoff notice we had recently received from the electric company. I guess he managed to pay all the other bills except this one. Another one of Dad's mess-ups. I began hammering everything in sight. I didn't even bother pushing my clothing out of the way, hammering through denim, cotton, and wool. I was like a shark in a feeding frenzy, unable to stop my own body. Completely out of control.

"Iris!" my dad yelled. I didn't know how long he'd been standing there, but I continued to pummel the walls.

"Iris!" he screamed again, this time grabbing my shoulders with both hands and physically pulling me out of the closet.

"Put the hammer down," he said.

I looked up and saw that it was raised above my head. Maybe he thought I was going to go after him with it. The truth was, in that moment, it had become like an extension of my body.

"You stole my money." I jumped right in.

"Wait a second," he said.

"No, Dad. Don't speak. You're always talking. Always lecturing me about doing the right thing and about how I've disappointed you. You're the one who said I've got to work through my anger management issues, and you know something—I have. I mean, I am working on them. But you! I think you're angrier than anyone in my program. Angrier than anyone I know! I mean, pretending to have a job? They say you're not even working there anymore. What happened to the promotion?"

"When I didn't get it, I quit. I was embarrassed to tell you."

I cut him off. "To steal money from your own daughter. Why do you hate me so much?" This was the question that had been brewing inside me for so long. It felt so good to let it out.

"I don't hate you, Iris." He looked defeated. "I hate that you think that."

I had said everything I wanted to say. And I said it without yelling. Or crying. Or feeling out of control.

"I didn't want to hurt you," he said.

"How did you think that taking my college money wouldn't hurt me?"

"It was just a loan."

"A loan is when someone 'loans' you something."

"I needed it for the house payment. Iris. We were going to lose the house."

"Maybe that's not the most important thing at stake here," I said.

We looked away from each other for what felt like an infinite amount of time. I thought about all the things he had done over the past couple of years to piss me off. The list was endless. I wondered how long his list was about me.

The sun was setting, and with no electricity, my bedroom was getting dark quickly. I opened my bedside drawer and pulled out some matches. I lit the few candles I had in my room. I almost laughed at the absurdity of having to have this difficult conversation by candlelight.

"Why did you get rid of all of her stuff?" I had wanted to ask him this forever.

Dad looked at me like I was broaching dangerous territory.

It didn't stop me. "I'm gonna talk about her, Dad. Just because she's dead doesn't mean we don't get to talk about her."

"I know that," he said, looking uncomfortable.

"So, tell me, why did you get rid of her stuff?" I asked.

"What stuff?"

"Everything. Her clothes. Her paintings." I scanned my memory to think of other things that hadn't made it to our move up north. "The card catalogue from the library."

"I didn't give it away," said Dad.

I was confused. "Well, where is it?"

"In a storage space, in Southern California. It's all there. Iris, it's hard to explain. I thought that I—that we—would heal faster if we didn't have so many reminders, you know? I thought if we could make a new life together, we'd be okay."

"She doesn't disappear just because she's dead."

"You're so right. How did you get to be so smart?"

"Definitely Mom's genes," I said.

He smiled. I hadn't seen him smile in ages. "I'm so sorry, Iris. I needed the money for the back payments on the house. My plan was to borrow the money, get a job, and put it all back there before you even noticed it was gone. It was wrong. *So* wrong. But I didn't want to disappoint you."

"How'd that work out for you?" I asked.

He stayed silent for a moment.

"I didn't want you to see your dad as a failure," he said.

These words sat in the pit of my stomach. My whole life I had worried about disappointing others, not living up to their expectations. These worries plagued me at night and propelled all of my decision making during the day. And here was a grown man, my dad, who acted like he had everything figured out, going through the exact same concerns.

Maybe I was more like him than my mom. I took a seat next to him on my bed. "So what have you been doing with all your free time? Besides stealing my money?" I had a right to know.

"Well, truthfully, the first few days were pretty bad. I spent them at a bar on Front Street. When I realized that wasn't helping anything, I decided to take that new suit I bought and put it to good use. I've been on the interview circuit for a while now. Something good will come along. I know it will."

"That's great." I thought back to all the fun times Mom and Dad and I had together. "We used to have fun, remember? We used to do things. I don't think you're a failure if you lost your job and can't afford our house anymore. I think it's more of a failure to ignore your child when she's already been left by her mother!"

Creases formed on Dad's forehead. "Mom didn't leave you."

"I was speaking metaphorically," I said.

"Iris. I'm not perfect."

No kidding.

"I don't know how I can say I'm sorry in enough ways to let you know I mean it," Dad said.

"It's not something I'm just gonna 'get over,'" I said.

"I know that. I don't expect you to. But can you try to forgive me?"

I nodded. What else was I supposed to do? I was tired of storming out of rooms and shutting people out.

I stared at the dusty pile of plaster, gathered like rubble after an earthquake, evidence of the anger that had passed through me—anger that I wanted so badly to disappear.

sixteen

Summer was almost over. In two short weeks, I'd be back at high school to begin my senior year. Instead of concentrating intensively on one class as I had this summer, I'd be bogged down with five classes, including organic chemistry (another AP science course) and calculus. Not to mention history, English 4, and Spanish 4.

I handed in my final paper with pride. I'd concluded it by asking readers to reimagine Little Red Riding Hood through the lens of Wolf-Alice. What would have happened if Red had taken the time to get to know the wolf? What had made him so vicious? Why was he a loner? How could understanding someone's history make one a more compassionate person?

I understood that we were all victims of circumstance, but, like Wolf-Alice, I didn't want to sit by and watch things happen to me. I wanted to be in charge of my own life.

With summer school completed, I tried my best to enjoy the only two weeks of freedom I'd have this summer. The lights were back on; I stayed in my pajamas until dog training on most days, sipped green tea from the teabags Oak had given me, and made a follow-up phone call to a woman who was interested in having me train her dog. She called back to say she was now away on vacation but would call me when she got back to set up a regular schedule.

On Saturday morning, the day of our Ruff Rehabilitation graduation ceremony, I slept through my alarm clock and received a jolt of adrenaline when I awoke and realized I had fifteen minutes to get down to Cliff Street. I threw on a black tank top and flowing skirt, knowing I'd have to hike it up above my knees when pedaling.

All the hard work over the last eight weeks culminated in today's graduation ceremony. I was so excited to see Roman, who had been "recovering" at Kevin's place from the trauma of being at the pound. He wasn't sure if Roman would be up for the graduation ceremony.

I pulled in to the Natural Bridges parking lot. Kevin was standing on the grass with everyone in our group in a circle. The dogs all sat in the center. We had spent the day before giving them baths and making them look perfect for the day they'd get to meet their new owners. Each day at dog rehab, I had done my best, but the whole time I wished the dalmatian were Roman. The night before, Kevin had let me know that freshly bathed Sid wouldn't even be at graduation, as his new owner had already adopted him and he was starting his new life in San Francisco. I was here to show my support for the other dogs.

After locking my bike, I made my way to the circle of dogs and their trainers. Oak moved aside, opening up the circle to reveal Roman in the center. Without hesitation, I bounded toward him, shouting his name. "Roman!"

He reacted to my voice right away and came sprinting toward me, his gait uninhibited by his missing appendage.

I slowly lowered my body down to his, not wanting to spook him, and let him lick the sweat off my face as I affixed the collar I had purchased around his neck. There was a certain look he was giving me, mouth agape, eyes glistening. If I believed animals could emote like humans, I could have sworn Roman was actually smiling at me.

Kevin gathered us together with our dogs and made the greatest announcement of all time.

"Every dog has been adopted out!"

"Even Roman?" I asked, concerned that he didn't count.

"Especially Roman," clarified Kevin.

We erupted in cheers and high fives as all the dogs' tails began wagging, our excitement contagious.

"We have about ten minutes until the ceremony starts, so just take some time to hang out with each other and your dogs for the last time. I'm gonna go make sure everything is okay with the graduation setup," said Kevin.

Oak came up to me and kissed me on my shoulder.

"Not here?" I asked, pointing to my face.

"I think your shoulder is the only spot Roman didn't lick," he said.

Before I could focus on Oak, I had to connect with Talbot. "Just a sec, okay?" I told him.

Oak held on to my hand. I could tell he didn't want to let me go. But if this was going to work, then he'd have to be the kind of guy who understood that having a best friend was equally as important as having a boyfriend.

"He hates me," Talbot said, after I let go of Oak's hand and went over to her.

"Not possible," I said. "Give it time. Guys can be like dogs sometimes—you just need to earn his trust."

"Well, I won't give up on being his friend then," Talbot said. It made me happy. I waved Oak over.

"You excited about today?" Talbot asked Oak.

I was relieved they were talking to each other.

"It's a great day. With some really good company," he said.

Oak leaned in and gave me a quick kiss on the lips. The butterflies in my stomach grew, but they were the good kind—the kind that helped me get out of bed every morning and face each day, instead of staying home and punishing myself, because I now believed that something good could happen.

Kevin came back to us. "It's a full house out there!" he said.

I wondered if my dad was in the audience—if he even bothered to come at all. I tried to tell myself that I didn't care whether or not he made it here on time, but the truth was, I wanted him to be there so badly. I wanted to show him what I had been doing all summer. I wanted to believe that he really cared about me as much as he'd said when we had our talk. And, mostly, I wanted to make him proud.

Kevin addressed the group. "Before we all get up onstage, I just want to tell you how blown away I am by the five of you for sticking this out, for being so successful in training your dogs. You inspired me, time and time again, over the summer."

I looked over, and Talbot was crying, which made me tear up. Even Randy was bowing his head so the bill of his baseball cap was covering his eyes; God forbid anyone see he had a soft spot.

Kevin continued, "Thank you for all of your hard work and dedication. I know these dogs can't talk, but if they could, I'm sure they'd say…"

"'I can't believe they let Talbot paint my toenails,'" interrupted Randy, pretending to speak as Garrett, who looked absolutely ridiculous sporting the pink glittery nail polish that Talbot had purchased. She had somehow convinced Kevin that the non-toxic nail polish would be the perfect and only way to send Garrett off to his new life.

When it was time, we made our official move to the makeshift stage (a large piece of plywood under a madrone tree). The audience was much fuller than I'd expected for a dog graduation, and I could see Talbot's parents in the front row.

It was noon and the hottest time of day. The sun's glare made it difficult to make out faces in the crowd. I sat with a program across my forehead, like a visor. As I scanned the audience for my father, who was not in attendance, I thought I saw Ashley sitting toward the back.

Had Dad even remembered that today was graduation day? I had been so hopeful after our big conversation together, probably too hopeful. I thought that he finally "got it" for once, but here he was letting me down once again. Maybe some people just weren't capable of changing.

Kevin welcomed the audience and began speaking about how we'd had a symbiotic relationship with the dogs; they helped us, and we helped them right back. Next, we did a short demonstration of everything we had taught the dogs over the summer, which included sitting, staying, rolling over, waiting to eat the food out of a bowl until we gave the command, not jumping up on people, barking on command (only about half the dogs could do that, and Roman certainly wasn't one of them), and fetching and retrieving. As I ran through these exercises, I thought back to the first time I tried simply to walk Roman on a leash. He'd pulled so hard, and I'd been timid; I truly had thought he was going to kill me. But as I looked down at him on our last day together, it hit me again how similar we both were.

We'd both been through so much in our short lives. Both of us were quick to anger, although Roman lashed out, and I kept mine inside. In truth, I needed to be a bit more like him, acknowledging and releasing my feelings as I felt them, and he needed to learn to be a bit more like me, not attacking everyone he perceived as a threat.

And this summer, we had both met our goals.

As Roman and I approached Kevin at the podium to receive my certificate of completion, my eyes locked on my father's face; he was sitting in the back. He hadn't forgotten about today. And what was more, his face was filled with pride, an expression that I hadn't seen on him in ages.

I took my certificate of completion and had a seat with the others.

Kevin was back at the podium. "And now, a bittersweet time for both myself and my fearless participants in Ruff Rehabilitation. We say good-bye to the dogs we've come to know and love as they say hello to a whole new future."

It was time to let go of our dogs.

Oak reached over and held my free hand. I was so happy to have him by my side.

Kevin called each dog and trainer pair up to meet their new owners, who emerged from the audience with great exuberance. First went Talbot, then Shelley. I watched as they each passed their dog along to their new owner.

Garrett went to a family of four.

Bruce went to an older gentleman who walked with a cane.

We were all shocked to see Sebastian, the Kite Boy, and his dad come up to collect Persia from Oak.

"What?" Oak said as he handed the leash to the little boy.

Sebastian's father stepped forward. "Ever since he met you guys, he's been bugging me about getting a dog. He wanted me to prove I like animals. This will be good for us. Thank you," he said, giving Oak a hug.

Tinkerbelle was next. Randy walked her to the front of the stage, and I watched the crowd to see who would emerge to claim her.

"Perry?" I shrieked when I saw my teacher take the stage. She didn't take the leash from Randy, who was holding it out to her, but instead picked up the dog and cradled her in her arms.

"We are going to have so much fun!" she said. She looked over at me and gave me a huge thumbs-up.

"You know her?" asked Talbot.

"Yeah, she's amazing!"

I was so happy for Tinkerbelle but secretly wished Perry had taken Roman home instead. Kevin had assured us that every dog had a new home, but what if the new owners backed out? Never showed up? Or worse—what if they were sitting there and were totally unimpressed with the way I had trained Roman? What if they felt the same trepidation that I'd felt on that first day of working with him?

My stomach tossed and turned with the returning fear that Roman would be put to death and it would be all my fault.

"And last but not least," Kevin began, "a dog with a long and complicated history, Roman."

Oak gave my hand one last squeeze before I stood up, with Roman heeling by my side, and headed toward the front of the stage. I looked out into the crowd. No one was walking toward the stage to gather Roman. The new owner wasn't coming. Roman would die.

I looked at Kevin, who read the panic on my face and pointed out into the crowd, where a man in his thirties was assisting a very pregnant woman up out of her seat. They walked slowly to the stage, and he held her hand, helping her up the stairs.

"This is Rashida and Jacob. This is Iris," said Kevin, introducing us. I went to shake their hands, but they brought me into a three-way embrace.

"I hope he likes babies," said Rashida, rubbing her bulging belly.

"He'll be great with kids," I said.

I leaned down to Roman. He looked at me with his big brown eyes. His eyebrows turned up and his head cocked to the side as if to question what was going on.

I petted him on the head and leaned down close to his ear.

"I love you," I said. "I always will. Be a good boy. These people are going to love you, too."

When I leaned in to give him one last hug, I felt him rest his head on my shoulder. I could tell he knew what was happening in that moment. He was telling me that he loved me, too. And the whole time I was thinking what a luxury it was to get the chance to say good-bye to somebody you love.

✿

After the ceremony, Perry found me in the crowd.

"These are for you," she said, handing me a bouquet of wildflowers.

"Thanks," I said, taking the flowers.

"That was a pretty special ceremony," said Perry.

"I'm so glad you're taking Tinkerbelle home."

"You know, I'm not supposed to be sharing this information with you until we officially file grades next week, but you wrote a knockout final paper. You got an A-minus in the class, Iris!"

"Are you serious?" I asked, completely relieved.

Perry nodded, her new dog at her feet begging to be picked up. Perry obliged.

"It's good to have a dog again," she said, kissing Tinkerbelle on the nose. "I have to run. We're headed straight for the pet store for another doggie bed—I want one in every room! Congratulations again, Iris. You've worked so hard."

"Thanks, Perry."

She turned to leave with her new dog. In the distance I could see Roman jumping into the backseat of the Volvo with his new owners. His tail wagging, he was excited for the adventure ahead.

"Hey, Perry!" I shouted out to her. "Are you teaching at SC High next year?" It would be amazing to have her as my English teacher senior year.

"No can do, I'm afraid. I'm strictly a summer hire. It's back to substitute teaching for me during the year. But hey, if your English teacher ever gets sick, I'm the girl to call."

Well, at least I knew there was no way they were ever going to give me Mrs. Schneider again.

Ashley ran up to me and gave me a huge bear hug.

"I'm so glad I came!" she said.

"Me, too." It was so good to see her.

"I can't believe I wasted my whole summer inside a coffee shop and you got to do this incredible thing!"

Ashley was right. What had started out as a punishment had turned out to be a gift.

I wanted more time with her. "Hey, want to join us at Lighthouse? We're all going for a swim."

"Sure! I'd love to. Just have to run home and get my suit. Should I invite Sierra? She leaves for college in three days."

I hesitated for a moment, wondering if we could go back to being who we were as a group, but I wanted to give them a chance to get to know the real me.

"Yeah, I'd like that," I said.

Dad sat back and waited for me to say my good-byes to my friends and to Kevin before approaching me. Dad was wearing board shorts, and his hair was slicked back, wet.

"You did great up there," he said.

"Thanks."

We looked at each other for a while—two people not knowing what to say.

"You smell like fish," I said, recognizing the saltwater smell on his body.

He nodded with a big grin across his face.

"You were in the ocean?" I asked.

"I needed to think. It's where she always did her best thinking. I thought I'd try it out."

"And? How did it go?"

"I found her today. In the water," he said.

I thought about how I had felt swimming in the ocean with Talbot. Mom had been everywhere then, and Dad had just experienced the exact same feeling.

"She's not gone," he said, trying to convince me.

"I know." I didn't know why it always took him longer to get things.

"I haven't been very good to you."

"Dad," I interrupted.

"No, hear me out. I acted like I knew everything, like my way was the only way. Like I was perfect. I'm far from it, Iris. I'm just slogging through who to be without your mother around. I was so focused on that loss that I took for granted the fact that you were still right here. I'm so sorry. I'm so very sorry."

And then my father did something I'd only seen him do once, on the day of my mother's funeral. He cried. And I did the only thing I could think of; I leaned in toward him and wrapped my arms around him and held him tight.

It was good to see him acting like a human rather than a working robot.

"I got a job," he said, when he finally calmed down enough to talk.

"You did? Where?"

"It's no big deal. I'll be shelving inventory at a bulk sale store on Ocean. The pay isn't great, but the hours aren't as crazy, which means I'll have a lot more time to spend with you, if you want to."

"I would like that," I said.

"And I'm paying you back, for everything. Every time I get a paycheck, a quarter of it is going to go to you. It may take some time, but I promise to have it all back to you."

"Thanks, Dad," I said.

"It looks like someone's waiting for you."

I turned to see where he was pointing. Oak was leaning against a cypress tree, watching us.

"Yeah, I should go."

"He looks like a nice dude."

"Dad, no one says 'dude' anymore, but yeah, he is nice. You'll like him."

"I'm real proud of you, Iris. Your mom would be, too."

I nodded and wondered if Mom would have gotten over her fear of dogs if she had seen me go through a program like this.

"I'm making dinner tonight. Cheeseburgers on the grill. You can invite your friend if you want."

"Can you make it veggie burgers?" I asked. I hadn't realized until that moment that since I started working with the dogs I had been avoiding consuming any sort of animal, and I wanted to keep it that way.

"Are you going vegetarian on me?" he asked.

"You should try it," I said.

"I just might do that," said my dad.

I couldn't believe that my choice might actually have an influence on the way he ate.

"See you later?"

"Yup," I said, giving Dad one last hug before joining Oak.

"That looked intense," Oak said.

"Beyond intense."

"You okay?"

"I will be." I put my hand in his. "Oh, by the way, are you good with spackle and a paintbrush?"

"I guess."

"Good, then you're coming over for dinner tonight," I told him. After we ate, I would ask Oak to help me patch up all of the gashes on my closet wall. These were my scars. It was time to let them heal.

"Oh, am I?" He pressed his body against mine and kissed me on the lips. A wonderful zing flew through my body. It was a feeling the opposite of rage, equally electric and overpowering.

"Ready for a swim?" I asked as he opened the passenger door for me.

"To the ocean, Ms. Moody."

I hopped in his car, and as we wound south along the cliffs, I looked out over the glistening Pacific, the endless ocean that made my world seem vast and unpredictable and full of possibility.

epilogue

It is the middle of February. I have planted myself in the corner of the library, wearing a wool sweater I bought in a secondhand store in Santa Cruz when I went back for winter break.

I'm not in Rhode Island but in Seattle, studying animal psychology at the University of Washington. It's not snowing out, as I'd hoped it would be in my library fantasy, but the rain falls in thick sheets, lulling me into a focused trance. If I allow myself to get distracted enough, I go through a running list of assignments I have to complete for my British literature course (I'm minoring in English).

Dad has a new job as a restaurant manager. It's not quite what he wants to be doing, but it's paying the bills, and each month, like he promised, part of his check goes straight to my savings account.

Oak is living in San Jose, working for some bigwig computer company. We're still seeing each other when we can, over my vacation breaks. He said he'd be able to come up and visit sometime in April, which really isn't too far off.

But mostly, when my mind wanders from cognitive behavior, it goes straight to Roman, whom I picture running along a beach somewhere, off-leash, sniffing the sand, dampening his nose in the ocean, and slowly learning to trust the world again.

Acknowledgments

Grateful acknowledgment is extended to my editors at Ashland Creek Press, Midge Raymond and John Yunker.

I'd like to thank each of these people for their part in helping me make this book: Andrea Quaid, Sheila Clark, Albert Mikulencak, Melissa Clark, Ron Clark, Lurie Strand, Lael Smith, and Lily Ng.

Special thanks to my husband, Basil, and my two boys, Peter and Phoenix, for their love, constant support, and enthusiasm.

The project was made possible in part by a grant from the Center for Cultural Innovation.

About the Author

Photo credit: Elizabeth Daniels

Jennifer Caloyeras holds an M.A. in English literature from Cal State Los Angeles and an M.F.A. in creative writing through the University of British Columbia. She is the author of the young adult novel *Urban Falcon*, and her short stories have appeared in a variety of literary magazines, including *Booth* and *Storm Cellar*. She is the dog columnist for the *Los Feliz Ledger*. Jennifer lives in Los Angeles with her husband and two sons. Visit Jennifer online at www.jennifercaloyeras.com.

Ashland Creek Press is an independent publisher of books with a world view. Our mission is to publish a range of books that foster an appreciation for worlds outside our own, for nature and the animal kingdom, for the creative process, and for the ways in which we all connect. To keep up-to-date on new and forthcoming works, subscribe to our free newsletter by visiting www.AshlandCreekPress.com.

Lightning Source UK Ltd.
Milton Keynes UK
UKHW040946290320
361022UK00001B/33